WARD STREET

The writer has authored another book entitled:

GOD HATE SIN...
BUT LOVES THE SINNER!

Melvin Mincey

MINCEY PUBLISHING HOUSE

Baltimore, Maryland

Copyright 1993

ISBN 0-9637969-0-9

Library of Congress Catalog
Card Number: 94-96019

MINCEY PUBLISHING HOUSE

WARD STREET

CONTENTS

```
About the author................I
The Testing Rod..............III
Acknowledgments..................3
Foreword.........................4
Jesse...........................15
Calhoun Johnson................20
Frederick Douglass.............31
Sweat, Funk, Snot And Tears....36
Jesse James Pritchard..........65
Calhoun Johnson Comes Home.....75
The Abortion...................83
Doctor Saltzman's Testimony...112
Doctor's Report...............123
The Ordination................154
The Dog Returns To Its Vomit..176
Reunion.......................208
Homecoming....................223
Doctor J.   ..................242
The Pro-life Activists........252
In His Presence...............266
Scripture Index...............276
```

***

WARD STREET

ABOUT THE AUTHOR

Melvin Mincey, the author, first of all is a born again Christian and a child of God. He is also a retired truck driver. He drove an eighteen wheeler for over thirty years.

He is also married to a wonderful woman, named Martha. He has two sons: David and Marvin.

The book, WARD STREET, was inspired by God. Without His wisdom and inspiration, the book would have never been written. God inspired men to write the Holy Bible. He inspire men to write today.

When God uses an individual to write His words, by His grace, He also allows the individual to express himself through his own personality.

The dominant purpose for writing, is to get the message through to the reader!

When we read the four Gospels: Matthew, Mark, Luke and John, we recognize that these four writers are telling the same story; but the story is told in a different way. Four different personalities.

WARD STREET

Whoever the writer maybe; or, whatever he or she may write about; everybody is not going to agree. But if a writer writes the truth and at least one precious soul is spared the agony of a Christless eternity in hell, the written word will have served it's purpose!

Melvin & Martha

WARD STREET

THE TESTING ROD

...Satan himself is transformed into an angel of light.
II Corinthians 11:14.

...If our gospel be hid, it is hid to them that are lost:

In whom the god of this world hath blinded the minds of them which believe not, lest the light of the glorious gospel of Christ, who is the image of God, should shine unto them.
II Corinthians 4:3-4.

Death...hell and destruction awaits those who allow themselves to be deceived by Lucifer!

Lucifer, that ol' serpent the Devil, and Satan, masquerades as an angel of light!

The description given of him by most artists and writers is false. If his appearance was as horrible and obvious as he is represented, he would soon be out of business.

Lucifer, is a created being. He was created by God. God is Omnipotent. Which means He is all Powerful! He controls everything.

"If that be so," one might ask. "Why is Lucifer allowed to run

WARD STREET

loose? Isn't Lucifer known as the deotroyer? If God has unlimited Power, why dosen't He rid the world of Lucifer?"

The answer to that question: "This life is a test!"

I believe Lucifer is being used as a testing rod!

In 1987, I had become angered about a certain matter, which I do not care to mention here. What is important is God's reaction to my anger. After the anger was over and my spirit subdued, God spoke to me verbally: **"THIS LIFE IS A TEST, TO MAKE SURE THAT WHO GETS INTO HEAVEN..."** He ceased speaking. For some reason He did not complete the sentence. I used my own words to finish the sentence: ..."IS FIT!"

A few years ago my mother died. When the undertaker finished preparing the body, he notified the family for a viewing. He wanted our final approval. When I stood there with the rest of the family where my mother was laid out, I remarked: "You know, if I didn't really know that this was our mother, I would never recognize her."

The undertaker had done his job

WARD STREET

well,but my mother had suffered a lengthy illness. My mother was always a heavy woman. But because of her illness, her body had deteriorated substantially. She was bearly recognizable.

I knew that my mother had lived a good Christian life, and was saved. When we walked away from the casket I concluded: that this life is designed to prepare one for a better life...for Heaven. If there is any sin at all in our members such as: hatred, resentment, lust, greed or pride;(especially pride); God has His way of bringing us to a place of total humility.Preparing us for Heaven!

In the Bible we read: **Before I was afflicted I went astray, but now have I kept thy word.** Psalm 119:67.

Who shall ascend into the hill of the Lord?or who shall stand in his holy place?

He that hath clean hands, and a pure heart;who hath not lifted up his soul unto vanity, nor sworn deceitfully.
Psalm 24:3-4.

***

WARD STREET

ACKNOWLEDGMENTS

I thank The Holy Spirit for guiding and urging me. I thank my Lord and Saviour Jesus Christ for helping me. And I thank God for being there in time of need. Without Divine help, I would not have been able to write this book.

> Dedicated to: Martha
> David
> and
> Marvin

Billy Joe Williams, the homosexual in this story, contracted the AIDS virus in an era when this particular disease was unheard of here in America.

Although he had acquried all of the symptoms which we now know as the AIDS virus, doctors and researchers had very little, or no knowledge of the disease.

The AIDS virus, according to researchers, seem to have it's origin in Africa or possibly in the caribbean.

However, the virus was not recognized here in the United States until 1981, while the disease had been causing death long before it was acknowledged.

WARD STREET

FOREWORD

The deterioration of the family unit has left our society devastated. Wherever there is disorder, social or whatever, sin lies at the root!

Society has attempted to teach moral values without religion, and of course it has failed. Society has allowed its children to grow up without any knowledge of what is expected of them according to God's Word.

All men, no matter what race, color or creed; how high or low; rich or poor, are made in the Image of God. All men are born with positive potential, for there is no respect of persons with God. But sin is a hindrance. Man, is far less than what God intended him to be. Man, should be thankful for the precious gift of life and seek not to use it for his own selfishness and pleasure, but use the gift to honor and glorify God!

Why boastest thou thyself in mischief, O mighty man? the goodness of God endureth continually. Psalm 52:1.

...Whatever ye do, do it heart-ily, as to the Lord, and not unto men;

Knowing that of the Lord ye shall receive the reward of the inheritance;for ye serve the Lord Christ.

But he that doeth wrong shall receive for the wrong which he has done; and there is no respect of persons.
Colossians 3:23-25.

The fear of the Lord is the beginning of knowledge: but fools despise wisdom and instruction.
Proverbs 1:7.

If we want a quadruple guarantee that we will never amount to anything, all we have to do is pursue foolishness and follow after vain persons.

Wisdom is the principal thing; therefore get wisdom:and with all thy getting get understanding.
Proverbs 4:7.

"What am I gon' be when I grow up?I ain't gon' be noth'n, 'cause my mamma don'told me so already!"

Dear reader, do the above words sound familiar to you? They are familiar. Yes, too familiar.

Parents do not have to actually tell children that they will never be nothing for them to live a wasteful negative life. Parents have only to tell them nothing. Even we as adults need words of encouragement.

A child, no matter how high the Intelligence Quotient, still think like a child, and need to be taught constructive principles to create a positive mind-set.

Be all you can be! Give life the very best you've got, with what you have to work with! All mankind need to heed these words persistently.

Every man, no matter what race or color, should be proud of who he is in spite of what others may say. If we do not feel worthwhile, we are saying that God made a mistake. The world tends to be extremely cruel when weakness is discovered in another. Unkind negative words can shatter every positive purpose that was ever there.

It is said, "A kind word to the afflicted and the willingness to associate with castoffs can turn a lump of coal into a polished jewel in God's Crown." Words can have eternal influence, for we who are here on the earth are being shaped for eternity!

WARD STREET

I must agree without reservation, with the words of Frederick Douglass: "The black race is a hated race."

Too many blacks hate other blacks. The murder rate is higher among blacks than anybody else.

The greatest bond of all is love. If mankind do not learn to love one another, there is not the slightest chance that we will ever see the Face of God.

Love bonds.

Hate, is an entity, which incorporates other entities such as envy, jealousy, malice, slander, division and strife. These are all attributes of war and murder.

Over thirty-five years ago, I happened to have been rambling through an old magazine whose publication had been discontinued. However, the magazine is in print again now. As I thumbed through the pages, I discovered an article which someone, after some sort of research I am sure, had printed. The reason for the article was to classify the different races. In other words, to determine the acceptance of one race over another; caste, which God hates! All men are made in the

WARD STREET

Image of God, so when we despise another, we are not despising man, but we are despising God.

The bottom line is, God does not make junk in any form. Man is His crowning creation made in His Own Image. No matter how loathsome someone may seem to us, God created him or her for Himself and for His Own good pleasure.

The Word says: **If a man say, I love God, and hateth his brother, he is a liar: for he that loveth not his brother whom he hath seen, how can he love God whom he hath not seen.**

And this commandment have we from him, that he who loveth God love his brother also.
I John 4:20-21.

If I had that old magazine at my disposal, I could make a more accurate report, but I have to do the best I can from memory. Right at the very top of the survey, was the white caucasian. Then from there, possibly every race in the world was listed which I cannot truthfully retrace in exact order but I do recall, that at the very bottom of that tabulation was the black race! Now, how the acceptance of all these different races was determined I do not know, but my guess is that many assumptions were made.

There is something that we as a people can do to pull ourselves out of this rut of negativism: live devout righteous lives, and teach our children to love and fear God.

The Book of Proverbs states: **Righteousness exalts a nation, but sin is a reproach to any people. Proverbs 14:34.**

This is what God said about righteous Abraham: **And the Lord said, Shall I hide from Abraham that thing which I do; Seeing that Abraham shall surely become a great and mighty nation, and all the nations of the earth shall be blessed in him?**

For I know him, that he will command his children and his household after him, and they shall keep the way of the Lord, to do justice and judgement; that the Lord may bring upon Abraham that which he hath spoken of him. Genesis 18:17-19.

Only take heed to thyself, and keep thy soul diligently, lest thou forget the things which thine eyes have seen, and lest they depart from thy heart all the days of thy life: but teach them thy sons, and thy sons'sons;

Specially the day that thou stoodest before the Lord thy God in Horeb, when the Lord said unto me,gather me the people together, and I will make them hear my words,that they may learn to fear me all the days that they shall live upon the earth,and that they may teach their children.
Deuteronomy 4:9-10.

The key to the abundant life which God intends for all men is obedience to Him.I do not believe that too much emphasis can be placed upon the negative circumstances that all men allow to dominate their lives.

The character about whom I am writing...Jesse Johnson, was born in a household where negative words were heard quite frequently. He had a mother who had lost confidence in her husband because of his careless lifestyle,and had developed a low opinion of all black men. Even though she was a good woman and a kind and loving mother, whenever she would reach the breaking point of frustration with Jesse's father,she would put

WARD STREET

Jesse down also.

Despite the fact that Jesse did not have a strong role model for a father; and in spite of the skeptical image of himself that his mother had injected into his spirit, he managed to live a fairly stable life for a while anyhow.

What kept Jesse's morale up was the presence of his aunt who lived in the same household...Sarah, his father's sister. Sarah was a strong Christian woman. She is who inspired Jesse to become a doctor.

Jesse was a good doctor and could have made a great contribution to the medical profession, but he made unwise choices. Living outside the law of God and man, he used his gift to abort unborn babies. His ego could not be pacified. Neither could his insatiable desire for wealth be satisfied. The reason why, Jesse did not have the ability to understand true values. He made the mistake of believing that a man's worth could be defined by dollars and cents, which is not true. Many of us I am sure, have observed men who had monetary wealth, but their

WARD STREET

worth beyond that did not amount to much.

Perhaps Jesse's mother was to blame, causing him to concentrate his priorities in the wrong place, seeking to pull himself up in the world any way he could. Whatever the reason for his conceit and greed, it caused his body to be destroyed on the earth and his soul in hell!

And whosoever shall offend one of these little ones that believe in me, it is better for him that a millstone were hanged about his neck, and he were cast into the sea.

And if thy hand offend thee, cut it off: it is better for thee to enter into life maimed, than having two hands to go into hell, into the fire that never shall be quenched:

Where their worm dieth not, and the fire is not quenched.

And if thy foot offend thee, cut it off: it is better for thee to enter halt into life, than having two feet to be cast into hell, into the fire that never shall be quenched:

Where their worm dieth not and the fire is not quenched.

WARD STREET

And if thine eye offend thee, pluck it out: it is better for thee to enter into the kingdom of God with one eye, than having two eyes to be cast into hell fire:

Where their worm dieth not, and the fire is not quenched.
St. Mark 9:42-48.

Without a doubt, all respect and support should be given to the dear Ministers, Lay people and others who are attempting to take our streets back from the dope dealers, thieves and murders, but I truly believe that we are trying to heal this malignant situation with a band-aid! You see, dear reader, when one has reached a level of depravity in which he or she is using or dealing drugs and will steal and kill to support the habit, the point of no return is probable.

Note, now, I did not place any emphasis on age here. We have in our society persons who have become corrupted from preteens on up. Their lack of respect for law and order is gaining momentum, but I believe if we do what is right we can end all of this.

Building more penal institutions will not remedy this esca-

WARD STREET

lating drain on our society, we have to program our children from the cradle. The younger the child, the more susceptible the mind to teachings, proper training and positive influences by which he or she is surrounded. Children need to be educated Spiritually and given every advantage so that their character may be formed into the Image of Christ!

I know without a doubt, that what I have said here is right. It is always proper to say and do what is right. I sincerely believe if we as parents do what is right concerning our children, within a few years it should make a difference! It takes only one transformed generation. All children deserve a chance at life. Parents have a responsibility from God to maintain the Spiritual life of their family through worship, devotions, prayer and service.

***

WARD STREET

CHAPTER-1

JESSE
Highlandtown

The rhythmical tone of rain drops dripping off the edge of the roof to an ol' tin can, and the syncopated beating of his heart, sent Jesse's imagination soaring into a surreal world of joy bells, as he stood gazing at the steady flow of traffic below, while it splashed through the rain soaked streets. The scent of fresh rain in his nostrils stimulated his senses back to reality, ushering his mind into the past. It is now Christmas Eve, December 24, 1986, and raining, the same as it was thirty-nine years before, back in 1947. Perhaps the similarity of the weather is what caused his thoughts to center upon that particular day in Highlandtown when he was just a 16-year old boy. He was playing football on a vacant lot, with five other boys his age.

It had begun to rain, and everybody went scurrying into an old shack located on a corner of the

WARD STREET

lot. Jesse was the only colored boy in the bunch, and he and his white buddies played well together. Segregation and jim-crow were quite prevalent in those days, but none of the boys seemed to notice.

While they waited for the downpour to let up, everybody made themselves as comfortable as they could. Richard, who was the self-appointed coach, found a wooden crate leaning against the wall. Securing it properly he sat down, sharing it with Jesse.

Jeffery, (Jeff, everybody called him), sprawled out on the floor next to Richard. Jeffery was a big husky 17-year old. He was the same age as Richard and loved playing football. Both boys were huge for their age, and preferred playing on opposite teams.

"Hey, Jeff," Richard said, ruffling Jeffery's hair. "What're you gonna be when you grow up?"

"The best linebacker there is," Jeffery answered, allowing a big grin to spread across his broad face. "What else?"

"That figures," Richard assured him. "You're already the best there is...right fellas?"

WARD STREET

Everybody agreed enthusiastically.

"What about you, Rich?" Jeffery wanted to know. "What're your plans?"

"Well," Richard shrugged his shoulders. "Guess I'll be like my dad...a doctor."

My mom wants me to go into the Ministry,"Christopher told everybody, getting up off the floor, after growing weary of being battered by rain drops dripping through a hole in the roof. "Mom wants me to be a Preacher, but dad keeps insisting that I play basketball."

Christopher, (nicknamed Chris), was a lanky 14-year old. He was younger than everyone else. Yet, he towered over everybody in the room at least a foot. He was better on the basketball court than on the football field, but played football just to be with the guys he liked.

"Yeah, but what do you want to be?" Jeffery shot at him. "What matters is what you want to do, Chris."

"Haven't made up my mind yet," Christopher drawled, thoughtfully. "Guess I'll have to though, 'fore

WARD STREET

I start college. I have a while to think about it yet. I'm sure I'll make the right choice when the time comes."

"I'm sure you will make the right choice," Jeffery agreed. "You are a good man."

Everybody turned their attention towards Jesse, questioning; but it was Harold who spoke up. "I like fix'n things. I'm working in my dad's shop already. I'm going to be a mechanic." He stuck his chest out matter-of-factly.

Harold was a tall 16-year old, same age as Jesse, who prided himself in working with his hands, as much as he loved playing football. Even while waiting there in the ol' shack, he was prodding up into the roof with a stick, over the spot where Christopher had gotten up from, trying to stop the leak.

Jesse got up off the crate, went and stood at the door and stared out into the rain, then turned towards his friends teary eyed. "What am I gon'be when I grow up? I ain't gon' be noth'n,'cause my mamma don' told me so already!"

Suffering from embarrassment, Jesse bounded through the door

WARD STREET

out into the rain,and ran towards home!

Jesse was a well built six feet two inch, two hundred and thirty five pound good natured boy. He was excellent on the football field,and considered playing professionally.

Jesse felt that it added something special to his appearance by wearing his cap backwards, and an earring in his ear.Despite the fact that his mother and his aunt Sarah insisted that he not look that way, he wore what he wanted to anyhow.

***

WARD STREET

CHAPTER-2

CALHOUN JOHNSON
Drunk And Disorderly

It had begun to rain harder now. Jesse was getting drenched, but in his present state of mind, he did not care. Attempting to shorten the distance towards home because it was growing dark, Jesse decided to take a short cut across a lot where most of the houses had been torn down.

Finding that he was wadding in a sea of mud, Jesse quickly scrambled back to the sidewalk, and stamped the sticky goo from his badly worn tennis shoes. He kept going until he reached Eastern Avenue. Turning west, he began the five mile hike to southwest Baltimore where he lived on Ward Street.

When he reached Highland Avenue the rain had nearly stopped. There was a big fat man on the corner dressed in a Santa suit. He filled the chilled evening air with jovial laughter and chatter, bringing joy to the expectant faces of the children huddled about him.

WARD STREET

Further down the street, a group of smiling faces were singing Christmas carols beneath the window of a neat little town house. A small boy with just a night shirt on, was waving from the candle lit window. When the carolers started moving on, the boy opened the window shouting Christmas greetings! The candle in the window, flickered once and went out, leaving the boy in the dark. Frightened, when he discovered that he was left without light, the boy cried, "Mamma!"

After a few more miles, Jesse was in his own neighborhood. Where he lived was far different from where his playmates lived. The old broken down weatherbeaten town houses with an outhouse attached, seemed to give evidence that this was the oldest neighborhood anywhere! The giant sized rats and the roaches did not make living there any easier either.

Then, Jesse was at the house where he lived. Even when he put the key in the lock, he could smell the aroma of good cooking. As far as he was concerned, his mother was the best cook in the whole wide world.

WARD STREET

His sister, Phoebe, was humming a familiar Christmas carol when he walked in. She was stringing lights on the tree."Hi ya,J.,"she said, cheerfully. "Merry Christmas!"

Jesse smiled, waved and kept on back into the kitchen.

"Where have yuh been, boy?" his mother, Ezzie Mae,wanted to know. She never looked up from the dough she was kneading for her pie crushes. "Yuh been gone all day! Where have yuh been?"

"Highlandtown...football practice," Jesse answered,running his finger around the rim of the mixing bowl sitting on the table, then sticking his finger in his mouth. "I've been working hard playing football."

"Your daddy is in jail, again, J.," his aunt Sarah told him,laxing her hands around the mixing bowl she was cradling in her lap. "A fine mess to be in right here at Christmas.We have been waiting for you to come home so you could go with us to Pine Street station to get him out."

"Go 'long wit'er, J.," Ezzie said. "Yuh'n Phoebe. I can't go. I have t'finish my cooking heah."

Ezzie put down the dough and cleaned her hands on the front of the apron she had on. She took the mayonnaise jar she kept her money in down off the ice box and shook the contents out on the table. She gathered the bills together and handed them to Sarah. "I don't know how much Cal's fine gon'be," she said. "Yuh better take it all. This is the money I was saving to buy everybody a Christmas gift wit'. Nobody will git anything now."

"Well," Sarah chuckled, setting the mixing bowl on the table. "Calhoun will sure get something; his freedom."

"What's pop in jail for?" Jesse wanted to know.

"Drunk and disorderly, as usual," Ezzie told him.

Twenty Five, Forty Five

"What can I do for you?" the sergeant asked Sarah when she stood at the desk with Jesse and Phoebe.

A glimmer of amusement twinkled in Sarah's eyes. "Do you have a

WARD STREET

guest here in your quarters name Calhoun Johnson?"

"Yes, we sure do," the sergeant laughed. "We always keep a room reserved for him. He's our best customer. Are you here to get him out?"

"How much is the fine?"

"Twenty five, forty five."

A few minutes later, Calhoun was following Sarah and his two children out of the police station. It was only a short walk from Pine Street to Ward Street, but Calhoun was still drunk and slowed everybody down.

They moped along quietly until Calhoun broke the silence. "I-I'm s-sorry," he stammered, lowering his head shamefully. "For...forgive me for causing trouble right heah at Christmas. I-I 'preciate wha'cha jus' done."

"We are your family, Cal," Sarah told him. "What did you expect us to do?"

"Aw, why do I have to be the one causing all the trouble? I'm disgusted with myself."

"We love you just the way you are, pop," Phoebe assured her father, slipping her arm around his waist. "We'll always love you."

"Yeah, we love yuh, pop," Jesse said, putting his arm around Calhoun's shoulders. "And it's good to have yuh home wit' us for Christmas."

"I don't deserve a family like I have heah," Calhoun sobbed. He took his hat off and shook his head. "I jus' gotta straighten my life out. Pray for me, Sarah. Pray for me."

"I've been praying for you for years," Sarah told him, cutting her stride back to where he was. "Now it's time for you to do something. Me and The Lord can't do it all. You have to do something for yourself. You have to make up your own mind to do what's right. We can't do that for you."

"Pop," Jesse encouraged. "Will yuh listen to aunt Sarah? She won't tell yuh noth'n wrong. She help's keep me straighten out."

"Yeah," Phoebe added.

Calhoun responded by shaking his head more hopelessly.

Jesse loved his father despite his faults. Although Calhoun had no formal education, he had a good mind. That is, when his brain was not saturated with cheap wine. Calhoun was a wine drinker...a wineo. Hanging out with the boys, (as he called them), had taken it's toll on his life. The boys, were the rest of the wine drinkers who hung out around south Baltimore.

Jesse hated to see his father live such a wasteful life. He recognized far better potential in him than his father realized himself. What was so painful, Jesse knew that his father had never given himself a chance at life. Jesse was aware that Calhoun had more natural abilities by accident than most folks had on purpose. He was well known around the neighborhood as the 'fix it man.' It was said, "If ol' Cal can't fix it, it just can't be fixed."

Jesse attributed his father's trifling inclinations to his good looks, and the fact that the women were constantly after him. Calhoun was a very attractive man. Ezzie shared with Jesse quite frequently the experiences she had when Calhoun was a younger man. "Yore poppa wuz sho' some'um t' look at back then." Then, she would chuckle, "'Course, I wuz never much t' look at, though. Maybe that's why the girls had the nerve t' 'proach Cal even when we wuz t'gether. They could'a thought I wuz his mamma or some'um."

Ezzie related to Jesse that not only did the girls flirt in her presence; they would actually attempt to coach Calhoun away from her. But of course, she would get mad and protect her rights as his wife. Over the years though, Ezzie grew weary and frustrated trying to defend her pride and womanhood. She learned to keep her cool. She would smile politely and say, "Thank yuh, fur admiring my man."

Jesse supposed, that his father would never lose his strong facial features, which displayed inescapable evidence of profound intelligence. The fiery eyes embedded in his handsome face still glowed with potential, although the light had been lessened by the abuse of strong drink, and only God knows what else.

Calhoun Johnson was not a religious man, but his sister, Sarah, was religious. It was said by everyone who knew her; if there

WARD STREET

were ever any mountains that had to be moved by prayer, aunt Sarah, (as everyone called her), could move them.

Sarah never married anybody. In fact, even though she was a beautiful woman and strong in character, she had never been seen with a man.

"Never had need for a man," was her reply, when asked about her love life. "All I need is my Jesus."

Sarah was not a religious fanatic, but she sure enough knew Who her Jesus was.

She was an exceptionally beautiful woman even with one eye partially closed. It was known that a man, (among many others who admired her), many years before when she was quite young and even more attractive, had physically beaten her badly because she rejected his unwanted advances and refused to marry him. The beating left her eye battered and partially closed. Calhoun and his friends, (against Sarah's wishes of course), sought revenge, and nearly murdered the man.

Ezzie was looking impatiently

WARD STREET

out the window when they arrived, and hurried to open the door. "Y'all got'im, I see." Shivering, she closed the door against the chilled night air,then turned her attention to Calhoun. "Yuh sho' gave us a nice Christmas. I hope yuh learned yuh lesson, now. Maybe this will make yuh straighten up!"

"I-I'm sorry, Ezzie," Calhoun blurted out, recoiling from her contempt. "I r-really am. Forgive me, please."

"Same ol' story," Ezzie snapped. "Same ol' broken record!"

Jesse came to his father's rescue by moving over near him with a look of defiance. He knew his mother, (mamma Ezzie he called her),loved his father,but she had lost respect for him.He also suspected that mamma Ezzie had lost respect, and confidence in all black men because of his father. Jessé supposed that this was the reason why his mother kept telling him that he would never be nothing.

Jesse had to admit that his mother was the backbone and bread winner for the family.She was the one who paid the rent and the

WARD STREET

rest of the bills, so that everybody could have a place to live.

Mamma Ezzie kept things going by cooking for a private family, and many times the only food in the house was brought home out of the white folks' kitchen. Aunt Sarah, of course, always paid her share of everything.

"Mamma Ezzie, don't yuh think pop should git some rest'fore yuh start fussn'?"

"Sho'! Go on put'im t' bed," Ezzie snorted, throwing up her hands hopelessly. "He ain't no good fur noth'n else. Go on...do some'um wit'im!"

***

WARD STREET

CHAPTER-3

FREDERICK DOUGLASS
Christmas Gifts

"Merry Christmas, J.," Phoebe whispered, brushing Jesse's ear with a kiss. "Merry Christmas. I have a gift for you. From me and aunt Sarah."

"Couldn't it have waited 'til later?"Jesse grumbled,turning his face from her. "Man...I'm still 'sleep!"

"I was too excited, J.," Phoebe said. "I know you'll like it.It's a book."

"A book? I don't want no book!"

"You'll want this book. I read one like it, already. It's about Frederick Douglass.This is a good book."

"Aw, Phoebe,lay it on the chair there." Jesse pulled the covers up more snug around his chin. "And git outa heah."

After Phoebe left the room, Jesse tossed and turned. He was dissatisfied because Phoebe had woke him up. "Why should Phoebe read a book about Frederick Douglass?" still grumbling."She's too

WARD STREET

smart for her britches already. I like her nerve...waking me up."

Jesse was unable to get back to sleep, so he got out of bed and went down to the breakfast table.

He greeted everybody, and his father got up from the table and hugged him.

"Merry Christmas, son," Calhoun said. "Sit down and eat your breakfast. Merry Christmas."

Jesse sat down at the table, filled his plate and started eating. It pleased him to see his father like this. If he did not receive any Christmas gifts at all, he would be satisfied just having his father home and sober.

Jesse sat at the table across from Calhoun beaming. "Sleep alright, pop?"

"Sort of," Calhoun shuddered. "More bad dreams than anything else. Dreamt I was still in jail, looking out through them bars." Calhoun held his fingers before his eyes making imaginary bars, and peered through at Jesse. "I've been looking like this all night."

"Glad we could git yuh out, pop. Bad to be in jail. 'Specially at Christmas."

WARD STREET

There were gifts under the tree for everybody, although much of the Christmas money had been used to bail Calhoun out of jail.

Calhoun painfully accepted his gifts, insisting that he did not deserve anything. "Why are you doing all this for me?" he protested. "I don't deserve this. You make me feel lousy." He blocked a tear on his cheek with his finger and brushed it away with the palm of his hand. "Ezzie...I'm gon' do better. I-I swear. I'm gon' get myself a job after Christmas. If God will only help me, I'm gon' get a job."

"Let us hope," Ezzie said doubtfully."

"And pray," Sarah added, showing no optimism. "Getting a job is one thing. Keeping it is another. So let us hope and pray."

Advisor to President Lincoln

Jesse was lying across the bed reading the book which Phoebe and Sarah had given him for Christmas. Phoebe came into the room and threw herself on the bed beside him.

"This is a good book," he told her, without taking his eyes off the page."Thanks for giving it to me."

"I told you that you would like it.Frederick Douglass was a great man."

"Yeah,he sure was.Imagine, born a slave. Yet, rising high enough to become advisor to the President. President Abraham Lincoln! Boy, I wish I could be like him!"

Jesse and Phoebe were interrupted when Sarah entered the room. "You can be like Frederick Douglass if you want to be," she told Jesse. "But of course you must have the right determination to do so.You've got to get up and get it. Study; learn; push yourself.Nobody is going to do it for you. Understand what I'm telling you, Jesse?"

"I think so," Jesse said, sitting up on the side of the bed. "Yuh'll have to help me, though. Show me what to do."

"First of all, Jesse, you have to learn to ignore your mother when she tells you that you will never be nothing. Your mother is a good woman and means well, but my brother has been such a disappointment, all of her confidence in colored men has been shattered! The next thing...learn to talk right. You will never get anywhere talking the way you do. You can do it. And please...do what Ezzie and me have been telling you to do; take that ridiculous earring out of your ear. And for God's sake, wear your cap right! You want to look like somebody, too!"

When Sarah left the room, Jesse sat motionless, pondering what she had said. Phoebe sensed that he wanted to be alone, so she left the room.

"Thanks, aunt Sarah," Jesse said under his breath. "Thanks. I'm gon'give life the best I've got!"

***

WARD STREET

CHAPTER-4

SWEAT, FUNK, SNOT AND TEARS
The Mourner's Bench

"Tomorrow is not promised to any of us!"the Preacher tried to convince everybody,when he ended his sermon. He stood before the congregation extending the invitation for Church membership. "The Scriptures say, behold,now is the accepted time; behold, now is the day of salvation. I urge you my brothers and sisters, think about what I am telling you.Don't delay any longer. Give your heart to Christ, today! He has the answer! He is, The Answer!" The Preacher became more persistent! "I warn you now! If you were to die this very moment without being saved, you would go out into a Christless eternity!"

As the Preacher talked about salvation and how important it is to accept it and be saved,Calhoun became submerged in an overwhelming flood of guilt. He was aware of his sins now.He was convicted.

This was the first Sunday in the year of 1948.Calhoun had come

WARD STREET

to Church with Sarah to prove to everybody that he could keep a promise. He wanted to make a better life for himself and his family by starting the new year right. First, he was going to join the Church. Then get a job and keep it. Now, here he was sitting in the Church Pew. Calhoun was sitting in the very last row, convicted by the Holy Spirit, and undecided what to do about it.

Sarah knew that Calhoun was not comfortable in Church. She had held his hand in both of hers since they had arrived. Now, Sarah could read the yearning in her brother's eyes, and she knew what he was longing for. She put her arm around Calhoun's waist and gave him an encouraging kiss.

"Let's go down to the Mourner's Bench," she whispered, and slid out of the Pew, taking Calhoun with her.

Sarah slipped her arm around Calhoun's waist again, and he put his arm around her shoulders, and both started towards the Mourner's Bench.

Half way down the aisle, they met Besse Moody. (Miss Bessie, everybody called her). Miss Bessie was

WARD STREET

a big three hundred pounder, who was a friend and neighbor of calhoun's family.

Bessie Moody had started shouting when Calhoun and Sarah first got up from where they were sitting, and was still shouting!

"Praise The Lord," she cried, smothering Calhoun and Sarah in the grasp of her heavy sweatie arms, before setting them down on the Mourner's Bench. "Thank you, Jesus! Thank you!"

Miss Bessie stood directly over Calhoun singing and clapping her hands, moving her big hips in a slow swaying motion. A lone tear slithered down Calhoun's cheek after clinging to his eye lid for a moment. Sarah dabbed at it with a napkin.

"Cal, I'm so happy for you," Sarah said, starting to cry herself. "Thank You, Lord, for saving my brother. Thank You, Jesus. Thank You!"

Reverend Cecil L. Williams strutted down out of the Pulpit to where Calhoun was, joined by the Deacons. While the Preacher was praying over Calhoun and the Deacons were trying to convince him of his need of salvation, Bessie

WARD STREET

moody kept shouting from one end of the Mourner's Bench to the other.

Finally, Calhoun scrambled to his feet and staggered up the aisle towards the door. Sarah stayed by his side steadying him. They both stepped out into the chilled winter air. Calhoun leaned against the side of the building nauseated, and wiping snot.

Sarah stood excited! "Did you get it, Cal? Did you get it?"

"Get...w-what?"

"Your religion?"

"Sarah, I couldn't get nothing in there! The funk was too high! Miss Bessie kept shouting all over me! I could bearly stand the smell. I'm sick. She made me sick. Phew! Let's go home."

When Sarah and Calhoun got home from Church, Ezzie eyed Calhoun suspiciously when they came into the house. "How did my husband make out in Church?"

"Well," Sarah sighed, plunging into a chair. "He didn't exactly get saved, but he gave it a good try." she kicked off her shoes. "Maybe next time, Ezzie Mae. Maybe next time."

WARD STREET

Calhoun tried to avoid Ezzie by going up stairs.

Ezzie stood with both fists propped on her hips."What hap'um, Cal?"

Calhoun had went half way up the stairway, but came back down where Ezzie was."Ezzie,I would've made out alright, but Miss Bessie kept shouting all over me. She shook funk all over that Church. Ezzie Mae...I swear! I had to get outa there! Whew! I'll never go back to that Church. I'll have to get my religion somewhere else. I swear!"

Ezzie glanced at Sarah in unbelief. "What hap'um, Sarah?"

"Well, Ezzie Mae, you know how Miss Bessie always shout when somebody goes down to the Mourner's Bench. She shouted when we went down there, too. Calhoun claims that the odor from Miss Bessie's body quenched The Holy Spirit. Ezzie, maybe he is telling the truth. Calhoun was sorta sick."

"Sorta sick? Sarah, I almost puked my guts out! Phew!"

"Aw-w-w, Cal,it wasn't that bad now. I was there, too, you know."

"Yeah," Ezzie added. "Yuh been

making all kinds of excuses t' keep from going t'Church. Now it's funk! What will yuh think of next?"

The revival

Two months had gone by since Calhoun's Unpleasant experience at the Mourner's Bench. He had sworn that he would never go back to that same Church again. Yet, he was there for the Revival. He had come to Church with Sarah, but she had left him waiting outside. Calhoun was trying to decide if he should go in or not.

The Minister who was preaching was not an eloquent speaker, but he was addressing the congregation with a convicting power such as Calhoun had never witnessed before. As he stood in the doorway The Holy Spirit convicted him. While standing there, Calhoun looked towards the Mourner's Bench and literally staggered against the door frame at what he saw. He tried intensely to control the flow of tears with the palm of his hands. Many of his ol' cohorts and drinking buddies were strewn across the Mourner's Bench with their heads bowed under deep conviction.

What made the impact so great, these were men and women whom Calhoun knew as hard and sinful. Those whom he considered more wicked than himself. Those Calhoun thought had passed the point of no return; drunkards, gamblers, thieves, liars, gays, whores and prostitutes. And, oh yes...he had known some to commit murder, too!

This Preacher, whoever he was, had the ability to draw many of the misfits out of the street into the Church, and even to the Mourner's Bench.

Billy Joe Williams, the Pastor's son, who was a bi-sexual, and seemed to be more woman than anything else, was sobbing uncontrollably. He was being consoled by his mother. Nellie Mae, one of the prostitutes who was also at the Mourner's Bench supposedly, grieving over her own sins was helping Billy Joe's mother console him.

Billy Joe was a good boy, or he had been until he strayed away from the Church. He grew up in the Church under the watchful care of his father and mother, but somehow he had chose to live a life of sin. Billy Joe sang on the children's choir when he was young. When he was older, he taught Sunday school. However, his Church attendance became obviously poor.

Billy Joe's parents warned him that whenever anyone leaves the Church, the only direction to go is down. He eventually stopped going to Church anyhow. For years he lived the life of a homosexual and male prostitute. Now he was back. Or, trying to come back to the Church. Anyhow, he was at the Mourner's Bench repenting. Sin, has a great magnetic inclination! Which makes the desire to return to the Church more difficult. The Devil and his crowd just does not give up that easily.

The Mourner's Bench was almost full, and before Calhoun realized what he was doing, he was not walking, but running down there himself. Suddenly, he was lying on the floor with his eyes closed. Strange sounding words were flowing out of his mouth. When he opened his eyes, Sarah was kneeling at his side, speaking in tongues also. Bessie Moody was shouting nearby. Now her presence did not bother him. Maybe it was because he had been slain in the Spirit!

Temptation

Blessed is the man that endureth temptation: for when he is tried, he shall receive the crown of life,which the Lord hath promised to them that love him.
Let no man say when he is tempted, I am tempted of God: for God cannot be tempted with evil, neither tempteth he any man.
But every man is tempted, when he is drawn away of his own lust, and enticed.
Then when lust hath conceived, it bringeth forth death.
James 1:12-15.
"No, definitely not!" Calhoun persisted, even though he was arguing a losing battle. "I ain't gon' go to bed with you no more. Not ever! I'm saved,now!Can't you understand that? God has saved, me!"
"Huh!" Nellie Mae sneered with an air of authority, flauting her well formed body before Calhoun's

face. "Calhoun, baby...if you were a rich man I would soon be a rich woman and you know it! You haven't been able to resist me all these years, I don't believe you will be able to resist me now."

Nellie Mae knew Calhoun was weak for her, and Calhoun admitted that she held power over him with her sexual behavior. He still made a fruitless effort to elude her. "Nellie Mae, didn't you get saved when you repented at the Mourner's Bench?"

"That's beside the point. I still have to make a living."

"You don't have to make a living selling your body!"

"It's all I know!"

"You still didn't answer my question. Did you get saved?"

"No!" Nellie Mae answered flatly, turning her back, then wheeling around sharply without warning kissing Calhoun full on the lips. A prolonged kiss which scrambled his senses and sent his heart racing with unexpected pleasure and desire.

Calhoun had come to Nellie Mae's apartment with sex the farthest thing from his mind. He had been sleeping with Nellie Mae for years, but his conversion had made the difference. He was at Nellie Mae's apartment because she had lured him there, under pretext of Bible study.

This was Saturday, one day before Calhoun was to be baptized. He had been looking forward to his baptism, but now, he was not sure. He never anticipated that he would ever feel the way that he was feeling now about Nellie Mae again, or any other woman. He loved his wife, of course. Calhoun was saved and knew it. Yet, within a few moments, he found himself wallowing in a sea of sexual pleasure, ecstasy and sin! The flesh, Nellie Mae and the Devil had won!

The Prince Of Darkness

"Cal! Yuh sho' yuh not gwine t' Church this morn'n?"

Ezzie Mae had come into the bedroom for the second time, trying to get Calhoun out of bed.

"No," Calhoun answered, avoiding Ezzie's intense glare. "I'm not going to Church."

"Is some'um wrong?"

WARD STREET

"No."

"Then why is yuh still in bed? Yuh ain't git'n baptized t'day?"

"Nah, I ain't get'n baptized," Calhoun replied, adjusting the pillow between his back and the headboard. "I changed my mind."

Ezzie sat on the side of the bed and made one last effort to convince Calhoun to do what she felt was right. "Cal. Yuh didn't look right when yuh got home last night. Yuh sho' there's some'um yuh ain't telling me? Yuh been up t' yuh ol' tricks agin?"

Calhoun finally gathered enough courage to look Ezzie eye to eye, and lie to her. "No, everything's alright."

He was guilt ridden for sleeping with Nellie Mae and giving her most of his paycheck, and wanted to tell Ezzie everything. He opened his mouth to confess, but nothing came out. He tried again...nothing! Calhoun concluded that it would be much wiser to just pray about it anyhow, for there are somethings that only God should know about. Confessing his sins to God instead of his wife would be more appropriate. God forgives sin, not his wife.

WARD STREET

"Ezzie, if anything ever goes wrong in my life again I'll tell Jesus about it. Ok? He'll fix it"

"He ain't gon' fix it if yuh don't git outa that bed and do what yuh sp'ose t' do. Why don't yuh c'mon an' git baptized? Me'n Sarah gon' be wit' yuh."

"Naw, Ezzie, it's wrong. I'll wait. Maybe next time.Next time."

Ezzie left the room without uttering another word. When Calhoun heard her leave the house with Sarah, he snuggled down into the covers and went back to sleep. Calhoun fell asleep quickly. But the Devil,the prince of darkness, dominated his dreams.

For whom the Lord loveth he chasteneth, and scourgeth every son whom he receiveth.

If ye endure chastening, God dealeth with you as with sons;for what son is he whom the father chasteneth not?

But if ye be without chastisement, whereof all are partakers, then are ye bastards, and not sons.

Hebrews 12:6-8.

The Devil never bothered Calhoun before,no matter who he had slept with,or whatever he had done.Now,

WARD STREET

the Devil was on his trail.

Calhoun found himself in a bowling ally. He rolled a ball down the lane knocking down the pins. A loud angry voice shouted back at him from behind the frame:**"YOU ARE WASTING YOUR MONEY!"**(Rebuking Calhoun for leaving half his paycheck with Nellie Mae).Immediately, the ball which he had rolled down the lane was whisked back at his head with such force,he bearly had time to dodge it. A man emerged from behind the frame and started towards him. Somehow,Calhoun knew that the man could not approach him from the right.

When the man crept to his left side and stopped, Calhoun was aware that he had encountered the most horrible creature ever! His appearance was awesome! A great gash was in his neck, and the wound was terrible,infectious and sore. His head was leaning off his shoulders as if becoming detached.

The scene changes, and Calhoun finds himself at the counter of a liquor store purchasing a bottle of his favorite booze. A door opens to the right, and the prince of darkness stands framed in the doorway.Calhoun recognizes who he is and fastens his eyes opon him. When Calhoun withdraws his attention, the Devil moved forward, angling from the right, slyly towards the left. The Devil stopped whenever Calhoun fixed his eyes upon him. He proceeded when Calhoun's attention was diverted.The next moment, he was at Calhoun's left side.

Suddenly, Calhoun was awake. Standing before him was the most handsome man he had ever seen, accompanied by three beautiful luscious women. The women were so dazzling, they were enchanting!

The man was dressed in a white tuxedo, with tails and tie. The women wore glittering evening gowns. The man was handsome, but his countenance was evil beyond description. Especially the eyes.

"Who...who are you?" Calhoun blurted out,startled."Who let you in my room?"

The man began to laugh with such intensity his entire body shook and trembled! The laughter was more of a howl and a shriek than anything else.His total personage delighted in this pleasurable moment. Except the eyes, which portrayed evil to stagger the imagination!

The Devil brought his laughter to an abrupt halt, conveying utter contempt in his countenance: "So, we are inquistive, now? Let me tell you who I really am...no, rather, allow me to introduce our dear ladies here. You are...quite a ladies man, as we all well know." Satan bowed courteously, nodded towards one of the women who came forth smiling, and took his extended hand, dipping her knees politely to Calhoun.

"This is, Ludita," Satan told Calhoun. "She's all yours, now."

Satan snapped his fingers, and in an instant Ludita was in Calhoun's bed in a mad swirl of erotic love! At the very height of Calhoun's sensationalism, Ludita's true character revealed itself.

"I am, Sexual Lust," she said, as she changed into the hideous demon which she really was, and leaped into Calhoun's body.

At this point Satan let out another screaming howl! He stopped just as sudden as before!

"This is, Grieda." He presented the second temptress.

Calhoun was more than eager

WARD STREET

now, and sat up in bed extending his arms longingly for Grieda. The sex scene was same as before. Just before Grieda entered Calhoun's body, she changed into a monster and told Calhoun her name was, "Sexual Greediness."

Satan chuckled gleefully, and brought the last seducer before Calhoun. "May I present Undra, the last of my beauties. She will be just as pleasing as the others, I'm sure." He let go with another hideous laugh!

Calhoun was like a wild man. He literally ripped the gown off Undra's luscious body before making love. But now, the love making was more painful than delightful. It transformed Calhoun into a state of insatibale passion!

Undra's transfiguration was more terrifying than the first two. She went into Calhoun's body letting him know that she was, "Sexual Unfulfillment!"

Calhoun was left screaming for mercy when the last demon entered his body. The more he cried out, the greater the thrill and exhilaration was for Satan. He laughed, jeered, and clicked his heels together until Calhoun passed out from pain and exhaustion. Disappointed, Satan took hold of Calhoun's limp form and tried desperately to shake him back to consciousness and the misery he so desired him to suffer.

Calhoun did not know just how long he had remained unconscious for he lost all tract of time, during his odeal with Satan. Ezzie and Sarah were at his bedside when he woke up. They were praying that God would save his soul.

When the unclean spirit is gone out of a man, he walketh through dry places, seeking rest, and findeth none.

Then he saith, I will return into my house from whence I came out; and when he come, he findeth it empty, swept, and garnished.

Then goeth he, and taketh with himself seven other spirits more wicked than himself, and they enter in and dwell there: and the last state of that man is worse than the first. Even so shall it be also unto this wicked generation.
Matthew 12:43-45.

While they promise them liberty, they themselves are the servants of corruption: for of whom a man is overcome, of the same is he brought in bondage.

For if after they have escaped the pollutions of the world through the knowledge of the Lord and Savior, Jesus Christ, they are again entangled therein, and overcome, the latter end is worse with them than the beginning.

For it had been better for them not to have known the way of righteousness, than, after they have known it, to turn from the holy commandment delivered unto them.

But it is happened unto them according to the true proverb, The dog is turned to his own vomit again; and the sow that was washed to her wallowing in the mire.
2 peter 2:19-22.

This I say then, Walk in the Spirit, and ye shall not fulfil the lust of the flesh.

For the flesh lusteth against the Spirit, and the Spirit against the flesh: and these are contrary the one to the other: so that ye cannot do the things that ye would.

But if ye be led by the Spirit, ye are not under the law.

Now the works of the flesh are

WARD STREET

manifest, which are these; Adultery, fornication, uncleanness, lasciviousness, idolatry, witchcraft, hatred, variance, emulations, wrath, strife, sedition, heresies,
  Envyings, murder, drunkenness, revellings, and such like: of the which I tell you before, as I have also told you in the past, that they which do such things shall not inherit the kingdom of God. Galatians 5:16-21.

Author's NOTE:
  Dear reader, I believe that one of the worst sins that we can commit against God and our own body is fornication! Yet, we do not often hear a direct attack against fornication from the Pulpit. Sin is warely mentioned from the Pulpit now-a-days, anyhow. Especially sex sins.
  I believe that it is a disservice to God and man, when a Minister allows his Parishioners to go to hell sitting in the Church Pew. In many Churches today, a member can live most any kind of loose worldly life he or she wants to, and will never get convicted by the Minister.
  I believe that when we commit

sex sins of any kind, we are opening the door to demonic powers. The sex partner we choose may be demon possessed. We have no way of knowing if a potential sex partner is possessed or not.

Let us see what the Scriptures have to say about the fornicator: **Know ye not that your bodies are the members of Christ? Shall I then take the members of Christ, and make them the members of an harlot? God forbid. What? Know ye not that he which is joined to an harlot is one body? for two, saith he, shall be one flesh.**

But he that is joined unto the Lord is one spirit. Flee fornication. Every sin that a man doeth is without the body; but he that committeth fornication sinneth against his own body.

What? Know ye not that your body is the temple of the Holy Ghost which is in you, which ye have of God, and ye are not your own?

For ye are bought with a price: therefore glorify God in your body, and in your spirit, which are God's.

I Corinthians 6:15-20.

In these last days, Satan is becoming bolder and bolder. If we

WARD STREET

really give some thought to why this is so, we will find that the Church is becoming weaker and weaker. The reason why is sin.

Sin within the leadership of the Church.

What I am writing here is the truth!

God does not lie!

God asked me one question which verifies all that I have said here: A few years ago I disobeyed God which led to sin. (All sin is disobedience to God, anyhow).

After the particular sin had ended in repentance, God asked me this question: **"NOW WHY IS THE CHURCH SO WEAK?"**

I did not have to ask, "Lord, what do you mean?" I knew what He meant!

Many of our young kids today knows that something is wrong. What I am sharing here just might be the reason kids are turning to satanic worship.

If you do not believe what I am saying here is the truth, check the book stores. The shelves are loaded with books on satanic worship. Do not take my word for it. Talk to the store managers. Our kids are buying those books! Book stores are selling more of those books than anything else! This is a tragic story!

The very essence of Satan is evil! He cannot love even when he is worshipped. He will destroy whoever worships him.

I believe that many of the murders which are occurring today are not just normal acts of violence in the sense which we may think of them. They could be sacrifices to Satan. He does require human sacrifice!

Our kids are disappointed because of what is going on in the Church. Plus the perverted, compromising life styles that their parents are living.

Whenever it is reported that a member of the Clergy has sodomized a child, or it has been proven that the Pastor of a particular Church is a habitual womanizer, it gives the Church a black eye.

A young child's mind is easily influenced. When the news media exposes a homosexual Pastor, or a Priest who are tampering with young boys, confidence in the Priesthood can become very discouraging.

I have another book that I

WARD STREET

wrote. The book is entitled: **GOD HATE SIN...BUT LOVES THE SINNER!** In this book I am coming down on the homosexual Pastors. Men who are pastoring well established Churches, with huge congregations. A member of one of these Churches read the book. After the book was read, he said to me later: "I see you have my Pastor in your book."

"Who is your Pastor?" I asked.

He told me.

"You being a member of that Church," I said. "I am surprised that you are admitting that your Pastor is a homosexual."

"We know what he is, "he said. "We love him. Whatever he is. We love him, anyhow."

The congregation of that Church should love this man. It is their duty to love him. God commands us to love everybody. But he should not be their Pastor. How can the blind lead the blind?

I am not God, so I cannot judge anybody. Only God has the right to do that. But one of the members who had been in this same Church for years, died. After his death, God revealed to me that his heart was not right when he died. This man was very dear to me.

WARD STREET

I believe that any member of the Clergy who has the authority to stand before a congregation, should take advantage of every opportunity to come against sin and the Devil with every aspect of his ability! And what do I mean by authority? When God has given him the authority! If he has been called to Preach!

If a Preacher has not been called, he is free to say whatever he wants to. He is only in the Ministry for whatever gain there is. But, of course, he wil pay the consequences later!

The Apostle Paul makes it quite plain right here: **And I brethren, when I came to you, came not with excellency of speech or of wisdom, declaring unto you the testimony of God.**

For I determined not to know any thing among you, save Jesus Christ, and him crucified.

And I was with you in weakness, and in fear, and in much trembling.

And my speech and my preaching was not with enticing words of man's wisdom, but in demonstration of the Spirit and of power:

That your faith should not stand

WARD STREET

in the wisdom of men, but in the power of God.

Howbeit we speak wisdom among them that are perfect:yet not the wisdom of this world, nor of the princes of the world,that come to nought:

But we speak the wisdom of God in a mystery,even the hidden wisdom,which God ordained before the world unto glory:

Which none of the princes of this world knew: for had they known it, they would not have crucified the Lord of glory.
I Corinthians 2:1-8.

The Scholarship

Jesse graduated from high school an honor student, and was given a scholarship to study medicine. Jesse had no money to pay for such an expensive education, so his mother and his aunt Sarah agreed that the gift had to have come from Heaven.

Jesse's father had failed to keep the promises he made at the beginning of the year. He could not be depended upon to help

WARD STREET

Jesse at all.

Jesse believed his father was sincere when he made the resolution, but somehow he was unable to become the asset to his family that he wanted to be. In fact, his father had become even worse than he was before. Jesse had no way of knowing that Calhoun was now possessed by demons.

Before, Calhoun's ruin was drink and unemployment. He did not drink anymore and he was working, but he had become more involved with Nellie Mae. Jesse had seen his father and Nellie Mae together a few times before, but it was never like this. He was now obsessed!

Finally, Calhoun left his family altogether and moved into Nellie Mae's apartment. Not only did Calhoun have a stronger fascination for Nellie Mae, but now he had a mad urge for all women.

In the months that followed, Calhoun could be seen cruising the streets of Baltimore, (especially Pennsylvania Avenue), in the ol' cadillac he now owned. He kept the ol' caddy loaded with women. Calhoun looked like something out of an ol' Al Capone satire, with the brim of his big-

WARD STREET

apple hat broke to the side, and a soggy cigar stuck in his cheek.

The cadillac was a 1938 white convertible. Although it was ten years old, it still looked new.

As the story goes, the cadillac was given to Calhoun by a numbers writer. Calhoun had hit the number and the man was unable to pay off the bet. In order to appease Calhoun and some of his ol' cutthroat buddies, he had given Calhoun the ol' caddy. Whether the cadillac completely covered the bet or not nobody could rightly say. Anyhow, the numbers man did not have to leave town.

Jesse did not see his father much anymore, but whenever he did Calhoun would peel a few bills off the roll he carried and stuff them into Jesse's pocket. Calhoun kept a big bankroll all the time now. And he did not seem to be working anywhere. He had quit the job that he had gotten earlier that year. Yet, he was more prosperous than ever. Whether it were numbers, drugs, or prostitution, it was not known.

After a while in medical school, Jesse's diction was much better.

WARD STREET

He cared how he wore his clothes now, also. Jesse discovered that when he made an effort to improve himself he was respected and accepted by his peers. It gave him self-confidence. He felt good about himself. His studies were exciting! Jesse discovered that probing into God's marvelous creation can,without a doubt,explain many unanswered questions. Yet, revealing more questions than answers. He soon realized that rigid research was always essential!

***

WARD STREET

CHAPTER-5

JESSE JAMES PRITCHARD
Phoebe's Pregnancy

"She is, what?" Jesse tried to convince himself that he had not heard Sarah right. "She couldn't be! Phoebe, pregnant? B-but, she's only thirteen!"

"She's pregnant," Sarah assured him. "It ain't no joke."

"J., I couldn't believe it either, 'til I took her to the doctor," Ezzie told Jesse. I believe it now. I don't know what we gon' do wit' that gal."

"Phoebe has been fresh for a long time," Sarah said. "And I'll tell you something else...she's been growing peach fur for a long time, too."

Jesse began speaking in a voice so low he could barely be heard, tapping each word out on the table with his finger. "Aunt Sarah, peach fur or no peach fur, Phoebe is too young to be getting pregnant!" Jesse raised his voice as he continued. "Who is, he? Who is, the boy...this man, that did this?"

WARD STREET

"Phoebe won't tell,"Ezzie said.

"O-o-oh," Jesse sighed miserably,laying his head on the table. He wrapped his arms around his head, as if trying to rid himself of the entire unpleasant situation by wishing it away.

Jesse had studied with all his heart so he could finish his education. Then, he would start working to help Phoebe with her education. Now, this!

After a short silence, Jesse raised his head and squinted at Sarah through wearied eyes. "Aunt Sarah, what was Phoebe's excuse?"

"Said, she loved him."

"Love? I can't believe this! In love! Having a baby! She's only thirteen...she's just a baby herself.My God! All the plans we had for her life...gone.Over.What can we do? What can...we do?"

Sarah shrugged her shoulders.

Everyone was bewildered!

Ezzie regained her composure first. "Maybe she kin finish school after she have her baby."

"Perhaps," Sarah said.

The Itch

WARD STREET

It was Saturday afternoon, nearly two weeks since Jesse had learned of Phoebe's pregnancy. He still had not gathered the courage to mention it to her.

He had laid down on the bed thinking about Phoebe and had fallen asleep. Now he was awakened by a commotion in the street below.

A crowd was gathered on the street across from his house, and was cheering and applauding as a man playing a mouth harp danced and wiggled around on the sidewalk. The man held the harp to his mouth with one hand, and he used the other hand to scratch his body all over. He was doing a dance called the Itch! The more consistent he was, the wilder the crowd grew!

Finally, he wiggled over to the edge of the sidewalk and spit into the gutter. He squirted a long stream of slime through the wide gap between his two big front teeth, slapping the cone side of the harp into his palm, repeatedly, beating out the loose saliva.

Phoebe stepped out of the crowd, moved gracefully over to his side and slipped her arm around his waist. The man put his arm around Phoebe's neck, wiped his mouth with the back of his hand and kissed her long and hard on her mouth. Both started across the street towards the house.

His senses scrambled, Jesse snatched his shirt off the back of the chair and put it on. "What was that?" he said aloud. "What the devil was that?"

He heard the front door open and close so he hastened down the stairs. When he reached the bottom of the stairway, Phoebe was standing there beaming. "J., meet Jesse James. Honey, meet my brother, J.; his name is Jesse, too."

Jesse grasped the man's hand politely. "So your name is, Jesse James, huh? Glad to meet you."

"Jesse James Pritchard," the man said, grinning contagiously. "How yuh doing, man?"

"O-o-oh," Jesse sighed. "I, see. Jesse James Pritchard. I'm fine. How're, you?"

Jesse took a step backwards to avoid the man's breath. Jesse James Pritchard was reeking with alcohol and was obviously drunk!

He stood swaying before Jesse, fumbling in the hip pocket of the

WARD STREET

bib-overalls he had on. He finally came out with a half pint bottle of white-lighting,(corn whiskey), and shoved it into Jesse's face. "Wanta drink, man?"

"Of course not. I don't drink. You shouldn't be drinking either. Especially going around with my sister. My sister is only a minor. How old are you?"

Jesse James Pritchard began unscrewing the top off the bottle. "Nineteen," he said.

"No, don't open that bottle in here. Nobody's drank a drop of liquor in this house since my father left. We don't drink here."

"Sorry, man."

Jesse James Pritchard obediently put the bottle back into his pocket, trying to organize his expressions.

Jesse stood sizing up Jesse James Pritchard rather disgusted. He was thankful that his mother was not there to witness what he had to. It was difficult enough to except the fact that Phoebe was pregnant. But to have her child fathered by such as this was even more painful.

Here was a man, who, without a doubt, had as much of a future as an ol' stray dog or an ally cat. Drunk; a pair of dirty overalls; his cap turned backwards,(the way he wore his own until he knew better),and Jesse doubted if this man even had good sense.

"Jesse James...do you have a job? Are you working?"

"Yeah,man.Sho' is," he stumbled down into a chair and crossed his legs."I work fur de city. Garbage truck. Good money. More'n I wuz making when I wuz din' home hauling pulp wood."

"Where is, down home? Where are you from?"

"North Car'lina...Green'bur.'"

"How did you meet my sister?" Jesse glanced at Phoebe, aiming the question at her also.

"We just...met, J.,"Phoebe volunteered. "In the street."

"Yeah, when I wuz working my route, "Jesse James added. "Phoebe's my girl."

"Just like that,huh?"Jesse queried, eyeing both of them incredulously. "My sister is pregnant and she shouldn't be. And all you can say is, 'Phoebe's my girl.'"

Stunned,Jesse James Pritchard's jaw dropped. His mouth was propped open, and he was speechless.

"You mean...you didn't know?" Jesse was surprised.

Phoebe had already begun to edge her way up the stairway to avoid the questions she knew would be coming her way. "I just hadn't told him, J.! I couldn't!" She broke down in tears, and bounded up the stair steps.

Jesse blinked after her in unbelief until he heard the door to her room slam!

Jesse James Pritchard stood up and started towards the door. "Hey, man, guess I'll be going."

Jesse was visibly irritable now, and Jesse James Pritchard was uneasy.

"What's your hurry?" Jesse asked. "Things getting too hot for you around here?"

"Jes' wanna be by myself, right now. Gotta git use t' de thought'a me being a daddy."

"Yeah, you do that," Jesse encouraged, ushering him out of the door. "Make sure you have a good story to tell my mother when you see her."

Jesse closed the door behind Jesse James Pritchard with a sigh of relief, shaking his head. He dreaded when his mother would have to meet this man and realize what Phoebe, her baby, had thrown herself away on.

Jesse had barely stepped away from the door when he heard the key in the lock, and his mother walked in and set two shopping bags on the floor. "Hi, J.!"

"Hi, mamma Ezzie."

Ezzie stood framed in the doorway, and looked Jesse over real good. "What's wrong wit' yuh, son? I don't see yuh looking like this much. What's the matter, J.?"

"Nothing."

"No. No, no. Yuh can't fool me, J.! Some'um is the matter. What is it?"

I met Phoebe's boy friend...her baby's father."

"Where? When did yuh meet'im?"

"Right here in the house. He just left a few minutes before you came in here. You should have seen him when he was leaving."

"I did meet some ol' straggly looking man right outside when I wuz coming in. I had no idea he wuz coming outa our house. I thought he wuz one of the bums from 'round heah. And he had the nerve t' wink at me."

Jesse turned his face away from

WARD STREET

his mother, concealing a snicker.

"Did yuh hear what I said, J.? That no good rascal winked at me, trying t' git fresh!"

"I heard you, mamma. I heard you. That was him alright. He was almost drunk, anyhow."

Jesse got up and stood by the window with both hands in his pockets, and stared out into the street. Then he turned back to his mother. "Mamma Ezzie, that dumb nigger don't have no class, no intelligence, no education, no nothing! What my sister seen in him I don't know. Maybe it's sex appeal. Yeah, that's it...sex appeal. Has to be. But of course, I am a man. Naturally I would never notice if he had sex appeal or not. How about you, mamma Ezzie, did you notice anything sexy about Jesse James Pritchard?"

"If there's anything sexy 'bout that man it sho' 'scapes me." Ezzie giggled gleefully. "Now if I wuz an ol' dog or some'um now, it might be a diff'rent story. Well, Phoebe's jus' a child, an'..."

Phoebe had crept back down the stairway unnoticed, and was leaning against the newell with her head lowered. It was quite obvious

WARD STREET

she had heard all was said.

"I love him anyhow," she said softly, her voice just above a whisper. "He was the first. He's all I know."

Ezzie got up from where she was and hugged her. "Yuh're only a child, Phoebe. Yuh'll soon git over this mess. After yuh have yore baby, yuh'll be able t' start living yore life agin like yuh sp'ose t'."

Phoebe started to cry on Ezzie's shoulder. Ezzie led her back up the stair steps and put her to bed. "I love yuh, Phoebe," Ezzie told her. "Yuh're still my child. My baby. Whatever comes outa this, I'll be still wit'yuh. I'll never let yuh down. God will never leave yuh either. He will always be there."

***

WARD STREET

CHAPTER-6

CALHOUN JOHNSON COMES HOME
Green Willow Street

Billy Joe was sitting on the steps whistling when Jesse got home from school. He got up when he saw Jesse coming and dusted off his pants behind, fanning his buttock with his hand.

"Hey, sweetie! How ya been doing? Gotta talk to ya, man!"

"'Bout what?" Jesse was very unimpressed.

"Ya father."

Jesse showed more interest now. "C'mon in the house." He opened the door and went in with Billy Joe on his heels. "Now, what's this about my father? Sit down, Billy Joe."

Billy Joe sat down on the edge of a chair, and put his knees together woman-like. "Ya father is in bad shape, J., I believe he's dying. Man...ya gotta go see 'bout'im."

Jesse slumped down into a chair across from where Billy Joe was, as if a great weight had pulled him down. "Guess I'll have to,

WARD STREET

Billy Joe. Thanks, for telling me about him."

"Man, you're my friend, J.! I was supposed to tell ya 'bout ya father. Ya don't know where he lives do ya?"

"Yeah, with Nellie Mae."

"He don't live with her no more. When he got sick she put'im out. Woman like that don't have no use for a man 'less he can do for her. Ya father lives alone on Green Willow Street. Near Pennsylvania Avenue where the fags and the prostitutes hang out at."

"Think he's there now?"

"I know he's there...can't go no where else. He's too sick to go anywhere by hi'self."

"Will you go over there with me, Billy Joe?"

"Yeah, I'll go with ya."

Jesse and Billy Joe walked from Ward Street to Pennsylvania Avenue. When they approached the Dreamland bar on the corner of Pennsylvania Avenue and Hoffman Street, the prostitutes began stepping out into Jesse's path trying to make a pickup. But they made snide, and slurring remarks at Billy Joe. Jesse shooed them

WARD STREET

off, and he and Billy Joe turned on Hoffman Street and hurried on over to Green Willow Street.

When they reached the house where Billy Joe said Calhoun was, the only visible presence of life was a dusty plant growing out of a flower pot in the window. Calhoun's ol' cadillac was parked at the curb with two flat tires and dirty.Jesse reached out to rap on the door of the house, but the door was opened part way already, so he and Billy Joe went on in. Jesse flipped the light switch on the wall but there was no power, so he opened the door wider to let in more light.

The house was musty, disorderly and dirty,with very little furniture. From the doorway they could see into the bedroom. Calhoun was lying on the floor near the filthy bed from which he had fallen, more dead than alive. He displayed a feeble degree of evidence that he was conscious of someone being in the house, but was too weak to respond. Tears clouded what little light that had crept into his eyes when he had recognized Jesse when they came into the room to get him off

WARD STREET

the floor and back into the bed.

Lips trembling trying to speak, and desperately attempting to raise his head, Calhoun agonizingly uttered one word: "J.?"

Jesse did not answer. He slipped the stethoscope out of his pocket and hung it in his ears. Placing the other end first on his father's chest, he listened with intensity. After moving the instrument to his lungs, Jesse listened again, then put the stethoscope back into his pocket. "We're taking you home, pop," he said. Jesse spoke very grave. And in the same tone turned to Billy Joe. "Stay here with him while I get a taxi."

Jesse left the room but decided to call his mother first, so he went around the corner to the Dreamland bar where there was a phone. The prostitutes and the faggots moved aside reluctantly as Jesse neared the phone booth. The prostitutes displaying their wares trying to turn a trick. The faggots grinning.

Jesse's mother picked up the receiver on the third ring. When Jesse heard her voice on the other end of the line, he told her about Calhoun.

Ezzie seemed unaffected by what Jesse told her about his father. If she felt any emotions at all, she kept them well concealed.

The Baptism

What man of you, having an hundred sheep, if he lose one of them, doth not leave the ninety and nine in the wilderness,and go after that which is lost,until he find it?

And when he hath found it, he layeth it on his shoulders, rejoicing.

And when he cometh home, he calleth together his friends and neighbors, saying unto them, rejoice with me;for I have found my sheep which was lost.

I say unto you, that likewise joy shall be in heaven over one sinner that repenteth, more than over ninety and nine just persons, which need no repentance.
St. Luke 15:4-7.

When Calhoun pulled up in front of the house with Jesse and Billy Joe, he had far more waiting than good food and a clean bed. The tender expressions which Ezzie exhibited; the inexpressible joy he read in Sarah's eyes, and Phoebe's unrestrained tears of gladness as they helped him out of the taxi, told him that he was more than welcomed home.

It was not until Ezzie and Sarah had put Calhoun's frail body to bed and had begun to bathe him there, (for he was too weak to be bathed in the tub), did they totally realize just how deteriorated his body had become. Sarah, who loved her brother so much, stayed prayerfully by his side.

When Calhoun gained enough strength to speak with something other than his eyes, he whispered feebly, "Sarah, I want to be baptized."

Sarah, compassionately, knelt weeping and praying. As she prayed, her thoughts went back when Calhoun was slain in the Spirit there at the Mourner's Bench. She never doubted if Calhoun had gotten saved, even though he had started backsliding the moment he left the Mourner's Bench. Satan destroyed his body, but God had saved his soul.

WARD STREET

Sarah got up off her knees and went down to the kitchen where Ezzie was. When she told Ezzie what Calhoun wanted, they embraced and shouted! Rejoicing!

Sarah went to the Phone and dialed her Pastor and told him about Cahoun's condition. Within minutes, Reverend Cecil L. Williams was standing at Calhoun's bedside telling Ezzie and Sarah that Calhoun was too weak to be taken out of the house. "We'll have to baptize him in the bathtub," he concluded. "He's so far gone."

Ezzie got Jesse to go out into the backyard and bring the big galvanized tub which everybody in the house used to bathe in. Jesse, with Billy Joe's help, filled the tub with water and helped the Pastor put Calhoun into the tub.

Finally, after being dipped and splashed by the Pastor and his two assistants, Jesse and Billy Joe, Calhoun was wet enough to be considered baptized. He came up out of the tub with renewed strength, filled with The Holy Ghost and shouting!

After he was subdued by everybody, Calhoun was put to bed. There was a peaceful calm in his spirit

WARD STREET

now that was not there before. When Ezzie came to his bedside with the medicine she had been giving him, Calhoun refused it. "I don't need it now," he said. "I'm healed Ezzie. I'm healed."

Within a few hours, Calhoun had gone home to be with The Lord.

***

WARD STREET

CHAPTER-7

THE ABORTION
Aunt Sarah's Advice

Phoebe was three months pregnant now, and was beginning to show. Jesse James Pritchard was in jail for killing a man with a straight razor for cheating in a crap game. Of course, Jesse knew from the start that this was an impossible relationship. In his opinion, Jesse James Pritchard was unfit to marry anybody, let alone his sister, Phoebe. Phoebe was too young to get married anyhow. Jesse concluded that Phoebe could not get married, and she could not have the baby either. The very thought of Phoebe marrying Jesse James Pritchard, or even having his baby was more than Jesse could accept.

Jesse James Pritchard could not be depended upon for child support, even if he were not in jail. What little money he had left over from his drinking was lost in the crap games.

Jesse knew without a doubt that abortion was wrong...murder; just

WARD STREET

as sure as taking a gun, aiming it and blowing someone's brains out! Yet, he considered it. Maybe, if he talked it over with his mother and his aunt Sarah first, it could make what he felt he had to do much easier. Phoebe's feelings had to be considered, of course. In fact, she would have to make the final decision. But Phoebe was so much in love with Jesse James Pritchard, she might be proud to be the mother of his child.

Dinner was over and everybody was sitting around the table making small talk. Jesse decided to present what was on his mind. When he mentioned abortion, Phoebe almost fell out of her chair. "What? I want this baby! No! This is my baby! What's wrong with you?"

Jesse tried to calm her down. "Take it easy, Phoebe. Get a hold of yourself. I thought you would feel this way. How are you going to take care of a baby? You are just a baby yourself. You have to finish your education." Jesse switched his attention to his mother. "Mamma Ezzie, how do you feel about abortion?"

Ezzie got up from the table and started clearing the dirty dish-

WARD STREET

es. "I ain't saying yes...and I ain't saying no. But one thing is fur sho', Phoebe don't need no baby.She can't ev'um keep her own room clean. I have t' do everything fur Phoebe myself. I ain't in no mood t' talk 'bout noth'n like this no how."

Jesse took Sarah's hand and held it tightly in his. "Aunt Sarah, I need your support in this. What do you say?"

Sarah squeezed Jesse's hand, letting him know that she sympathized with the situation. Her tone of voice projected the same feelings.Jesse knew that whatever his aunt had to say,would be said in honesty. "J.," she said. "You should know better to even ask my opinion concerning an act of sacrilege. When we destroy something as sacred as a human life, God is being mocked! If we murder another human being,which is made in the Likeness and Image of God, we are showing contempt towards God and He will hold us accountable!This is a terrible thing that has happen here, J.; and I know just how inconvenient it has made everything for everybody here,because I am a member of this family, but abortion is not the answer. God is the Answer. That's one of God's little creatures Phoebe is carrying around inside her. If we take it out and kill it, it will be murder. Some folks claim that they don't know when life begins. But they do know. We all do. Especially you, J., you are a doctor. You haven't finished school yet, but you have learned enough to know that life begins at conception. Why are you allowing Satan to deceive you like this? Forget this nonsense and let Phoebe have her baby."

Jesse withdrew his hand from Sarah's as if she had just become contagious, and squimed around in his chair uneasily."Something has to be done, aunt Sarah. Something has to be done. Whether you agree with abortion or not, we have to do something with that baby. We all know that marriage is impossible here, so if you can come up with anything else other than abortion, you let me know. I will be glad to listen"

Sarah got up and started helping Ezzie with the dishes. "All our lives are in God's Hands,"she said. "He knows what's best for

WARD STREET

everyone."

Phoebe left the kitchen and went up to her room, followed by Jesse.

On the way to Phoebe's room, Jesse stopped in his own room and picked up his stethoscope. He went into Phoebe's room and sat on the side of the bed where she was lying and examined her. "The fetus seems to be healthy enough," he said. "The heart-beat is normal. You still can't have this baby."

"J.!"

"Phoebe, do you believe I love you?"

"Yes, but..."

"I would give my life for you if I had to. You believe that, don't you?"

"Yes."

"Then why don't you trust me? I know what I'm doing. Look, I will do the abortion myself."

"I don't know, J., I love this baby, already. Anyhow, what would mamma and aunt Sarah, say?"

"What difference does it make what they say? You are the one that's got to have this baby. Besides, mamma Ezzie is undecided anyhow, and I don't think she even cares."

WARD STREET

"She cares alright. Mamma would never go for nothing like this. I know she wouldn't."

"Phoebe, if you have this baby you will have to quit school and take care of it. You know what it's like going through life without an education. You will be just another drain on the welfare system. Do you want to work in the white folks' kitchen for the rest of your life like mamma? Think about what I'm saying. You need an education. You need to be free."

Phoebe sat up on the side of the bed and began to cry. Jesse took her in his arms and encouraged her. "Phoebe, tell you what; nobody has to know about this. I'll go see Billy Joe, and see if we can use his place for a few hours. Okay, ol' buddie?"

Phoebe nodded her head without looking at Jesse, and he started for the door. Jesse paused in the doorway, turned and clinched his fist, giving Phoebe the victory sign. Then, trotted down the stair steps.

The Arrangement

WARD STREET

Billy Joe was visibly upset when Jesse told him what he wanted his apartment for. Although he was bi-sexual and had slept with many sex partners, both, men and women, his way of thinking had been changed. He had been converted. The Holy Spirit had done His work there at the Mourner's Bench, and he had been wonderfully and gloriously saved. God had healed him of his homosexuality. He was straight now...born again! Even his appearance had begun to change: hair style, form of dress, the way he walked, speech and mannerisms. He was becoming more masculine.

In times past, (during Church services), when the Preacher would address the congregation on Men's or Women's Day; asking all the men to stand on Men's Day; and requesting the same of the women on Women's Day, Billy Joe was indecisive. To clarify vacillation, he would stand with the men on Men's Day. Then, stand with the women on Women's Day. God had changed all that now. He knew his true identity.

It was quite obvious to Jesse that Billy Joe had reformed, so when he refused to allow him to use his apartment for what he wanted, he did not attempt to persuade him. In fact, Jesse was rejoicing in his spirit because of the change in Billy Joe's life style. It was a great contrast to the perversion he once lived in: homosexuality, male prostitution, orgies, and every other sex sin imaginable.

Billy Joe was hated by both, the homosexual community, and the prostitutes. He was a well sought after professional. An all time favorite in the business. Therefore, they had to accept whatever was left...or what he did not want.

Jesse left Billy Joe and told him that he was on his way to see Nellie Mae. Maybe she would help him.

"Nellie Mae is born again, too," Billy Joe told him. "I doubt if she will help you take an innocent life. Nel, is not the same Nel you once knew."

Nellie Mae opened the door for Jesse and embraced him when he came in. "What are you doing in my part of town, J.? Long time no

WARD STREET

see. I'm glad to see you. How have you been?"

"I'm doing fine. But I'm slumming right now." Jesse laughed, and kissed Nellie Mae. "How are, you, Nellie? My, you look swell. Change in your life?"

"Born again. Sit down, Jesse."

Jesse sat down and crossed his legs. "I just left Billy Joe. He told me that you had made a change in your life. I'm glad for you, Nellie. You've come from a long ways. Nellie, I haven't seen you since my pop's funeral. Tell me, what happened between you two, anyhow?"

Nellie Mae sat down and reclined into the Chair. "Jesse," she said. "I've made a lot of mistakes in my life, but your father was the biggest one. He really didn't know what he wanted. Especially the women. I gave him love. Even sold my body for him. Still, that was not enough. So when he got sick, I put him out. Of course, had I known the Lord the way that I know Him now, I wouldn't have done that," her voice grew tender, "I would have taken care of him. I loved your father, J., and I loved him a lot."

WARD STREET

There was a moment of silence; Jesse gave Nellie Mae time to lament. Then, he told her that he needed her apartment.

Nellie Mae was puzzled. "Why would you need my apartment?"

"First of all, my sister, Phoebe, is pregnant."

"Yes, I know that."

"Then, you know she can't have that baby. I have to abort it."

"What? And you want to use my place? You want my help? No! Are you out of your mind? You can't do a thing like that!"

"I have to."

"You don't have to do no such thing!"

"Nellie, I need your apartment for just a couple of hours."

"No! Do you think I'm crazy? I won't do it! No!"

Jesse got up and strode to the door. "I'll have to go some place else, then."

"Wait a minute, Jesse." Nellie Mae got between Jesse and the door. "Sit down, Jesse. Just for a moment."

Jesse propped his hand against the door frame. "Yes?"

"Don't you harm that girl. Come on back over here and sit down...

please. I want to talk to you."

Jesse sat down where he was before, and Nellie Mae stabilized her equilibrium. "Alright," she said."If you must do it,I'll help you. But only to keep you from taking that child some place else and harm her. You see, it's like I told you, J.; I loved your father. I love his children, too, and I don't want anything to happen to either of you. I've had some training as a nurse, so I will be able to help you.When can you bring her over?"

"Tomorrow night,if it's alright with you. And, Nellie...thank you for what you are doing.I love you for it."

"No, Jesse, don't thank me for helping you do this, because my heart is not in it. I am doing this for only one reason...I believe that I can take care of Phoebe better than anybody else."

The Curettage

Jesse had no trouble getting Phoebe out of the house. Telling his mother that he was treating

WARD STREET

Phoebe to a movie, they left and rode the trolley over to Nellie Mae's house. When they got there Nellie Mae was peering out of the window, and eagerly opened the door and let them in. She anxiously embraced Phoebe, kissed her and made her at ease. "How is my little girl?" she said. "It sure is good to see you."

"Hi," Phoebe said.

Nellie Mae turned her attention to Jesse. "Bring everything, J.?"

Jesse set a little black bag on the table. "In the bag. A curet. That's enough."

"That should do it," Nellie Mae said. She opened the bag. "No anesthetic?"

"Couldn't get none. I'm not a licensed doctor yet, you know. there'll be a little discomfort for Phoebe without it, but she'll be alright."

"Phoebe." Nellie Mae put her arm around her. "Do you want to go through this without an anesthetic?"

Phoebe nodded her head.

Nellie Mae glided her into the bedroom and prepared the bed.

Jesse went into the bag and brought out the instrument he was

WARD STREET

to use for the abortion.

When the bed was ready, Nellie Mae stripped Phoebe naked and put one of her own night gowns on her. Nellie Mae's night gown was far too big for Phoebe and hung loose and clumsily on her body, but they made use of it anyhow.

Nellie Mae took Phoebe's pressure. She called Jesse into the bedroom and gave him the nod. "She's ok."

Jesse hugged Phoebe and kissed her before starting to work on her, hoping to build her courage.

Brushing a tear from her cheek, Phoebe told Jesse that she loved him, and trusted him.

Jesse recognized from the very beginning the great risk involved, and the tension was obvious to Nellie Mae. She watched uneasily, steadying Phoebe as she squimed around on the bed from the pain, as Jesse probed with the curet.

Nellie Mae assisted as best she could, nervously wiping perspiration from both Jesse's brow and Phoebe's body.

After a few minutes the abortion was over. It had seemed an eternity to all three; Jesse, Nellie

WARD STREET

Mae and Phoebe.

Jesse assured Nellie Mae that all the fetus, afterbirth and amniotic sac had been cleaned out of the uterus and told her to prepare Phoebe to go home. Nellie Mae suggested that Phoebe should have something to eat and rest awhile before she went home, and brought hot soup from the kitchen along with two tiny pills, and a glass of water. She stuck the two pills into Phoebe's mouth and told her to swallow them with a sip of water. Phoebe took the pills but refused the soup.

An Act Of Mercy

O Give thanks unto the Lord;for he is good: for his mercy endureth for ever.
Psalm 136:1.

Five days had gone by since the abortion and Jesse had brought Phoebe home and put her to bed. Yet, she still had not come down from her room. Both, Jesse and Phoebe realized that the excuse which Jesse had given mamma Ezzie and Sarah for keeping her in bed,

WARD STREET

was becoming suspicious. Jesse had been lying to Ezzie and Sarah, telling them that he was treating Phoebe for a virus. When Phoebe's condition began to worsen, he feared they might discover the truth.

The training Jesse had received as a medical student enabled him to diagnose the seriousness of Phoebe's condition; that she was becoming infected and was in need of far better care than he had available there in the house. He was quite aware that she needed hospital treatment, but fearing what he knew the doctors would find there, he continued to use the limited training he had himself, to make her better.

Since the curettage, bleeding had never stopped, and Jesse became panicky. So after a few more days, he decided to tell his mother the truth. He told her about Phoebe's condition, but lied about the abortion. He said that Phoebe had suffered a miscarrige.

"And yuh tried t' keep some'um like this from me!" Ezzie scolded Jesse. "Why didn't yuh let me take care of my baby, boy? Yuh know better'n this!"

WARD STREET

Jesse's heart was aching and it showed."Mamma,we just didn't want to worry anybody. I'm sorry."

"So this is why yuh wuz washing Phoebe's clothes and bed things. Trying t' hide all this from me. Making me think yuh wuz doing all that just t' help me out!"

Jesse made no comment, in an effort to attract less attention to himself as possible.

Ezzie called Sarah, and they went with Jesse to Phoebe's room. Ezzie and Sarah had gone to the room everyday to care for Phoebe, but somehow she and Jesse had managed to conceal the real cause of her suffering.

When Ezzie and Sarah came into the room with Jesse trailing behind, Phoebe knew by what was written on their faces that what she and Jesse had been so careful to keep hidden was now known."Oh, my Lord, mamma," she cried. "I didn't want you to know about this! I didn't want you to know!"

The scene in Phoebe's room was one to behold; Ezzie holding Phoebe in her arms lamenting aloud, rocking to and fro as if Phoebe were still an infant; Sarah kneeling at the bedside with

WARD STREET

hands and eyes raised towards Heaven weeping, speaking incoherently, praying in tongues! Jesse was pacing the floor, wringing his hands and shaking his head as if undecided what to do next. Then, he reasoned that the most sensible thing was to call the ambulance and have Phoebe taken to the hospital.

Ezzie rode in the ambulance with Phoebe. Sarah and Jesse followed in a taxi.

At the hospital, Phoebe was rushed into emergency where a team of doctors began working on her. Ezzie, Sarah and Jesse waited with apprehension and anticipation in the waiting room, until Ezzie heard her name called over the sound system. Then she reported to emergency as instructed. When she entered the room, one of the doctors moved grimly away from Phoebe's side. "Ezzie Mae Johnson?"

"Yes."

"I'm Doctor Saltzman." He nodded towards Phoebe. "Let's talk about her."

Ezzie, tearfully said, "Yes?"

"Follow me."

The doctor took Ezzie into another room and motioned her to a well cushioned chair, then sat down behind the desk. "Tell me," he said. "Who butchered that girl like that?"

Ezzie drew herself to the edge of the chair. "B-butchered? What do you mean, butchered?"

"Yes, butchered. That child in there is lucky to be alive. Who's responsible for this?"

Ezzie eased back into the chair again. "Yuh see, Doctor, my daughter had a miscarriage and she didn't tell anybody..."

"Miscarriage? Oh, no! No, no! There was no miscarriage. This child has had an abortion. I thought you knew."

Ezzie propped her mouth opened. "You...you didn't know."

"But...but, but why didn't they tell me? How could they do this t' me? I'm their mamma! J., should'a told me 'fore he did this."

"Who's J.? Is he responsible for this?"

"J., is my son. He did this. Well, Doctor, I reckon I'm just as guilty as he is. When he first started talking 'bout this kind'a mess, I didn't agree, and I didn't disagree either. Might be why he did what he did."

"How could your son even attempt such a thing without really knowing what he was doing. I want to talk to him."

"It ain't as bad as it looks, Doctor. My son has had some medical training. He's going t'school now t' be a doctor."

"Mrs. Johnson, medical training or not, he still had no right to do this. Let us get your son in here."

Ezzie left the room and came back in a few minutes with Jesse. "Doctor Saltzman," she said. "This is my son, Jesse. J., this is Phoebe's doctor."

"Hello," Jesse said.

The doctor stood and extended his hand. "Jesse, so you want to become a doctor? Sit down, son." The doctor pointed Jesse to a chair. Then, sat down himself. "Jesse, you have gotten your sister in a bad fix. Why did you do it? Couldn't you have thought of something else? That girl could have had that baby, and she could have still been healthy. What do you have to say about what you have done?"

Jesse shifted around in the

chair uneasily, and cleared his throat. "You see, Doc., my sister is very young. Her life hasn't even started yet. Plus, the man that fathered that child is no good. I had to do something."

"Yuh didn't have t' do this, J.," Ezzie spoke up. "Yuh didn't have t' make a mess like this! Yuh almost killed my child!"

"Abortion is serious business," the doctor added. "You could go to jail. However, if your sister pulls through alright,we will try to keep you out of jail."

Jesse blushed. "I don't care what happen's to me, now. I want Phoebe to be alright."

"We will try and make sure that she will be alright. Jesse, the reason you had problems after the abortion,you didn't know what you were doing. The abortion was incomplete. That is why the child lost so much blood, and infection set in."The doctor relaxed,placed his finger tips together and aimed them at Jesse."J.;...mind if I call you, J.? Your mother does."

Jesse forced a smile and nodded.

"J., in order to do a complete abortion after a prolonged preg-

WARD STREET

nancy, a curet should be used to scrape the uterus. If..."

Jesse interrupted."Doctor,I did use one of those...a curet."

"Oh, you did. As I was saying, if the uterus is not thoroughly cleaned, continuous bleeding will occur, and infection will set in. Fortunately, we do have proper drugs...antibiotics, to bring the bleeding and infection under control.But in this particular case, you may have waited too long before you brought the patient here. We will do whatever we can to save her. J., you said you did use the proper tool to do the curettage. I am sure that you are not aware that part of the fetus was left in the uterus."

Jesse shook his head. "No."

"It was. That is what caused the bleeding and infection." The doctor paused, and continued. "Of course,had you brought her to the hospital sooner,she wouldn't have had to suffer so."

Jesse readjusted himself in the chair."I knew she was in a lot of pain,but I didn't think it was as bad as it was. I took care of her the best I knew how. Doctor, the reason I didn't bring her to the

WARD STREET

hospital sooner, I didn't want anybody to know about this. I realize now it was a mistake."

"If yuh had'a told me," Ezzie said emphatically. "I could'a took care of my baby, and she wouldn't have had to suffer so bad. Yuh know, Phoebe might make it and she might not. My baby's sick in there."

The doctor stood up. "Let us hope and pray that she does make it," he said, and smiled at Ezzie. "You can go now. We'll keep Phoebe for a few more days. If we need you we will call you."

Agnes Taylor and Bessie Moody were sitting on the door steps when they got home. Ezzie got out of the taxi first, and trudged over to where Agnes and Bessie were, leaving Sarah and Jesse paying the taxi fare.

"How did y'all make out?" Agnes anxiously questioned Ezzie. "What hap'um, Ez?"

"Plenty," Ezzie puffed. "Pray fur us."

Bessie Moody's eyes grew wide. "Phoebe is alright, ain't she, Ezzie?"

WARD STREET

"She's alright fur now," Ezzie sighed. "We'll just have to keep trusting in The Lord."

Agnes Taylor got up off the steps and took Ezzie by the arm. "Anything we kin do, Ez? Me'n Bessie is yuh friends. We gon' hep yuh anyways we kin."

"Yeah, we been buddies a long time, Ezzie Mae," Bessie Moody said, rubbing her hand up and down Ezzie's back. "When you hurt we hurt."

"I know, I know," Ezzie groaned, sitting down where Agnes had gotten up from as if anxious to get a heavy load off her feet. "Y'all won't let me down. I love y'all, too. We'll always be that way. I'll come git yuh if I need yuh."

"Ez." Agnes was frowning, looking as serious as she could. "What hap'um t' dat gal anyhow...causing'er t' be so sick?"

"Well..." Ezzie lowered her eyes. "J. got rid'a that young'un she wuz carrying and almost killed my baby. She's some kind'a sick."

"What? Why would J. wanta do some'um like dat? Having chil'in is a honor. Bringing chil'in in't de worl' brings glory 't God!"

WARD STREET

"Miss Agnes." Jesse had gotten out of the taxi with Sarah following. "What you just said about having children are true. That is, if the mother happens to have a husband. Phoebe has no husband. Not even a decent father for her baby. Not only that, she's too young to be bringing children into the world. She's just a baby herself."

Agnes stepped over to the edge of the sidewalk and spit out a mouthful of snuff juice into the gutter, and wiped her mouth on her apron. "J., yuh oughta be ashamed o' yuhself..."

"No, Miss Agnes," Sarah interrupted. "You are the one who ought to be ashamed...bringing thirteen children into the world, and nary a husband. Didn't you have any pride about yourself? How could you do such a thing? All those children, and you have never been married to anybody!"

Agnes Taylor started grinning. "Yuh know, Sarah. It made my spurtongue feel good when I was git'n dem chil'n. It sho'..."

"Aw-w-w, Miss Agnes, please. Show us some respect! There is something in the world besides

WARD STREET

sex. Try thinking about something else for a change. Please do that."

Agnes spit again, licked her lips and laughed aloud."Yak, yak, yak, yak! It feels good git'n chil'n,Sarah.'Course,yuh wouldn't know noth'n 'bout dat, would yuh? Yuh never had a man! O-o-oh... yak, yak, yak, yak..."

Agnes Taylor left a trail of laughter behind her as she strutted on down the street towards her own house, with Bessie Moody treading on her heels shaking her head hopelessly.

Ezzie, embarrassed when Jesse shot a sensitive glance at her, got up and went into the house to avoid any uncomfortable questions.

Jesse switched his attention to his aunt. "Aunt Sarah, what on earth is a spurtongue?"

Sarah chuckled."You see, Jesse, what Agnes calls her spurtongue, is really her clitoris. You are a medical student. You should know what a clitoris is."

"I know what a clitoris is. But a spurtongue...spurtongue. I have never heard that one before."

"J., it's a wonder Miss Agnes

hasn't lost her mind. I suspect she will one day. All she talks about is sex. Maybe she's like that because she's older now and the men don't notice her the way they did once."

"Well, aunt Sarah," Jesse giggled."There's one thing for sure, somebody did notice her. She's got thirteen children to prove it."

Sarah laughed in agreement, and they went into the house where Ezzie was.

The telephone was ringing persistently and Ezzie motioned for Jesse to answer it, complaining that she was too tired to move. Jesse lifted the receiver off the cradle and held it to his ear. "Hello," he said. He listened. Then, took the receiver and the cradle over to where his mother was. "The hospital," he told her.

Ezzie sat motionless while she listened. Then, the receiver crashed to the floor as it slipped from her grip. Her mouth started to twist and tremble. She tried to speak but was unable to.

Sarah realized that the news Ezzie had received was dreadful, and rushed to her aid. She first made Ezzie as comfortable as she

WARD STREET

could and left her in the care of Jesse, with his little black bag and stethoscope. Then, Sarah reluctantly picked up the receiver from where it had fallen, and began to speak very quietly into the mouth peice."Yes? is this the hospital?"

"Is everything alright over there?" came the response on the other end of the line. "I heard a crash."

"No, everything is not alright. My sister-in-law is in a terrible state of shock. What did you say to her?"

"This is Doctor Saltzman,Phoebe Johnson's doctor. I'm sorry. I am so sorry. I was just telling Phoebe's mother that Phoebe died a few minutes ago. We did all we could to saved her, but she died soon after her mother left the hospital."

Sarah became unstabled, wept secretly. Then, regained her strength."Doctor, I'd better call the ambulance for my sister-in-law. I'll talk to you more about Phoebe when we get to the hospital."

The neighbors, including Agnes

WARD STREET

Taylor and Bessie Moody, gathered in front of the house when Ezzie was put in the ambulance. Ezzie's mouth was completely distorted now, and she was scarcely recognizeable.

Agnes and Bessie, both crying profusely, insisted on riding in the ambulance with her. The ambulance, with siren screaming, roared away from the curb with Jesse and Sarah following in the car with their neighbor, Mr. Bud. Mr. Bud was driving the same ol' cadillac Jesse's father owned when he was alive. Jesse's mother had given the ol' caddy to Mr. Bud when Calhoun died.

Ezzie arrived at the hospital and was rushed to the emergency room. The doctors perservered but she could not be revived.

Everybody was silent and grim when they rode home from the hospital with Mr. Bud, grieving over the sudden loss of two loved ones.

"It's better this way," Bessie Moody said, breaking the silence. "I believe this is God's act of mercy. I just can't imagine Ezzie having a stroke and living the

WARD STREET

rest of her life crippled, not able to do for herself. I believe this is God's way of relieving her of all her burdens and pain. First, her husband ran off with another woman. Then, came back home sick and died. On top of all that, Phoebe got herself pregnant and ended up dead. Too much...too much on Ezzie. She couldn't take all that! It was just too much!" Bessie Moody's heart broke. She cried aloud! Her big chest shook and heaved, with broken uneven sobs.

Agnes Taylor dabbed at her eyes, and blew her nose. I'm gon' miss ol' Ez. We been buddies a long time. It ain't gon' be de same 'round Ward Street wit'out'er. I'm sho' gon' miss'er."

***

WARD STREET

CHAPTER-8

DOCTOR SALTZMAN'S TESTIMONY
Time To Think

Several weeks had gone by since the double funeral. This was the day that Jesse was going to court for the hearing concerning Phoebe's death. As he sat at the breakfast table across from Sarah, pondering, he was uncertain which emotion he felt was the most prevalent; the annoying sense of guilt or the dreadful state of depression. Jesse was suffering from an overwhelming awareness of guilt because he was responsible for Phoebe's death. He believed that his mother would still be alive if it were not for his error. He was depressed because he was lonely without both of them.

The food on his plate went untouched as he allowed his mind to gratify itself, with the precious moments he had shared with Phoebe and his mother. He rejected condemnation entirely, relishing in the private chambers of his imagination.

WARD STREET

"It's getting late, son," Sarah told Jesse. "We had better get ready to leave here if we are going to meet the judge on time. We are in enough trouble already. We don't want no more."

Sarah's interruption shattered the recesses of Jesse's mind, crumbling his temporal wall of self-justification! Now, he was more disillusioned and apprehensive than before. He got up from the table, scampered up the stairs and got dressed. Jesse was aware that he had become more convicted and debased than ever!

When they entered the courtroom Jesse immediately recognized the doctor who had attended Phoebe at the hospital...David Saltzman. The doctor had seemed friendly at the hospital and smiled a lot. But now, he was more solemn. Doctor Saltzman never took his eyes off Jesse from the very moment Jesse came into the courtroom.

Jesse was glad that he had his lawyer in the courtroom, for he had become uneasy. When the doctor went up to testify, he was more than eager to take the oath and begin answering the questions that the prosecuting attorney and Jesse's lawyer inquired of him.

In the testimony, the doctor stated that Jesse's license to practice medicine could not be revoked for what he had done, because he never had a license to begin with. And the reason for that, he had never finished medical school.

Doctor Saltzman concluded by telling the court that, in his opinion, Jesse should never be issued a license to practice medicine. And that, he would do all within his power to keep him out of the medical profession.

Jesse's lawyer, of course, defended him as best he could, but Jesse was given eight years for manslaughter.

While in jail, Jesse used the time to think; to ponder his aspirations, disappointments and failures. What ultimately shattered his dreams of ever achieving his highest goal, were the words of Doctor Saltzman there in the courtroom.

Jesse wanted to practice medicine beyond anything else he wanted to do. Now, his hopes and

WARD STREET

dreams were gone! What kept Jesse from living in a state of total hopelessness, was his aunt Sarah's frequent visits and prayers.

Sarah continually told Jesse that he could still accomplish whatever he wanted, despite the circumstances against him.

Whenever Sarah failed to come to the prison on visitor's day, Jesse would become depressed. And today was one of those days that he felt as if the entire world was against him. Sarah had not visited him for some time now. He was quite certain that she had good reason not to, but still, it did not make him feel any better.

Then, the guard was at his cell unlocking the door telling him he had visitors. When the guard brought Jesse into the visiting area and he saw Sarah and Nellie Mae through the screened partition, tears burned hot against his eye lids.

They tearfully embraced as best they could, touching hands and cheeks on opposite sides of the screen.

"Hey-y-y, are you, J.?" A tiny but persistent voice came from below. "I want to get back there

WARD STREET

with J.!"

In answer to Jesse's inquisitive reaction, Nellie Mae reached down and lifted the little fellow with the voice face to face with Jesse. "Hey, are you, J.?"

"Yes, I'm J.," Jesse chuckled. "Who're you?"

"Rodney! Hey...I like you, J.! What are you doing back there,J.? Why can't you come over here with us?"

"Well, it's like this..." Jesse started to explain, embarrassed.

"Can we come over there?" Rodney wanted to know.

"Hold on there, little fella," Sarah told Rodney,taking him from Nellie Mae's arms, planting a big kiss on his forehead."Give us all a chance to say something."

"I want to be back there with, J.," Rodney insisted. "I want to be back there!"

"Where did that little guy come from?" Jesse laughed. "He is sure making my day."

Sarah stood Rodney on the floor and put his hand in Nellie Mae's. "Isn't he something for a three year old?" she said."Nel,will you take him somewhere so I can talk to J.?"

WARD STREET

Nellie Mae led Rodney towards the waiting room where the vending machines were. Rodney was still chattering!

Jesse grimaced, and clutched at the screen. "Aunt Sarah, I never thought being in jail would be as bad as this." He took a tighter grip on the screen. "I will be more than glad to get out of this place. It is hell in here."

"I know, I know," Sarah said, sympathizing with him. "We'll do all we can to get you out of here...Nellie Mae and me. You have a life to rebuild and live. I still want you to practice medicine."

"Do you still think I can become a doctor, aunt Sarah? Have you forgotten what Doctor Saltzman said about stopping me?"

"Doctor Saltzman may do all he can to stop you, but we will do all we can to help you. Doctor Saltzman is only a man. There is still a God in Heaven...He's running things. If He wants you to become a doctor, that's what you will be."

A gleam of light glowed in Jesse's eyes...hope! "I'm praying that you are right, aunt Sarah.

WARD STREET

I'm praying that you are right."

"I believe God is going to send you back home soon. I'm there all alone now. It's lonely there without you. Nel and Billy Joe will be living with me soon. They are getting married."

"What? Billy Joe marrying somebody? Billy Joe and Nellie Mae?"

"They're engaged. I meant to tell you before now. They'll be getting married soon."

"What's Nellie Mae going to do about Billy Joe's sexuality? He's almost as much woman as she is."

"Hey, aunt Sarah!" Rodney was coming back with a mouth full of bubble gum, dragging Nellie Mae along behind. "Watch this bubble!"

Sarah smiled and took him in her arms again.

"Hi," Jesse said, amused. "You again. You didn't stay away long, did you?"

"Hey, J.," Rodney persisted. "Look at this!" he produced a well inflated balloon like bubble which exploded after a few seconds and clung to his face, and his clothes.

Nellie Mae began the task of cleaning Rodney off as best she could, rebuking herself for buying him the bubble gum in the first place. "Lord, gimme strength," she concluded. "This boy is a nuisance. I don't know if I should adopt him or not." She laughed and gave Rodney a big hug.

Jesse eyed Nellie Mae incredulously. "You are...adopting him?"

"If I can. He has no father or mother that's any good. His father is a Puerto Rican, and his mother is Miss Agnes Taylor's daughter. They are both drug addicts. How they ever had such a smart child as this I'll never know. Rodney is only three, and already he's a genius."

"Hear that, J.?" Rodney shouted. "I'm a genius!"

"Aw, c'mon," Jesse laughed. "You are not a genius. You just talk more than anybody else."

Rodney tugged at Nellie Mae's hand earnestly. "Nel, ain't I a genius?"

"Watch your diction, now," Nellie Mae corrected him. "'Aren't I a genius.'"

"Aren't I a genius, then?"

"Yes, you are a genius. Now be quiet so somebody else can say something...please?"

"Yeah, ol' buddie," Jesse said.

WARD STREET

"Button your lip."

Rodney rolled his lips tightly together and bit down hard with his teeth sealing his mouth, and stood erect, as if standing at attention.

Jesse turned to Nellie Mae. "Nel, is it true that you are marrying Billy Joe?"

"Yes."

"But, he's a bi-sexual. A homo!"

"Was."

"I believe, once a homosexual, always a homosexual."

"He's alright. He's straight now."

"Are you, sure?"

"Yes, I'm sure."

"I hope you are right, Nel. Now that I've thought about it, the last time I saw Billy Joe he did look and act more masculine. The change was really noticeable. I had forgotten about that. Maybe you are right, Nel. I hope so for his sake, anyhow. Homosexuality is so disgusting...a waste of manhood."

"He has changed. If he hadn't I would never consider marrying him."

"God has fixed him," Sarah injected. "When God fixes you, you

WARD STREET

are fixed. I've been talking to Billy Joe and praying with him, too. He is not the same Billy Joe we once knew. But there is one thing for sure, if he ever turns back to his sin, he will be worse than before."

The guard moved over to Jesse and told everybody that visiting hours were over.

Sarah smiled at the guard humorously. "Are you sure your time is correct, officer?"

His glance and his body language convinced Sarah that his time was correct.

"We have to go, J.," Sarah said. "We hate to leave you, dear. But our time is up."

"Aunt Sarah, please don't stay away as long as you did before," Jesse told his aunt. "It's lonely in here."

"I won't, dear. I'll visit you once a week if I can. Every day if I could."

"I'll be back, too, J.," Nellie Mae promised. "I won't forget you."

"Thanks, Nel," Jesse said. "You too, aunt Sarah."

Sarah and Nellie Mae embraced Jesse again and prepared to go.

WARD STREET

"What's wrong with Rodney?" Jesse chuckled. "He keeps pointing at his mouth. I think he wants to say something."

"Can I open my mouth now?" Rodney muffled. "I want to say good-bye, to J., too."

Nellie Mae lifted Rodney off the floor up to where Jesse was. Rodney put his lips to the screen and kissed Jesse good-bye.

***

WARD STREET

CHAPTER-9

DOCTOR'S REPORT
Charlotte

Nellie Mae had decided that she wanted to be a June bride, and the day of the wedding was perfect for the occasion. It was a sunny, breezy, Saturday afternoon, with great white billowy clouds floating around the edge of the navy blue sky. And the temperture was just right.

The Church was full. The crowd emptied out into the street. It seemed, as if everybody in the neighborhood had turned out to see Billy Joe and Nellie Mae do their THING, as many had maliciously remarked. When one end of block was opened to let the limousine in to take Billy Joe and his bride-to-be to the entrance of the Church, the crowd shifted to the sidewalk. Much of the crowd consisted of old cohorts and associates, such as: bi-sexuals, faggots, lesbians and prostitutes; relationships which Billy Joe and Nellie Mae had severed when they changed their life-style.

WARD STREET

Nellie Mae was a beautiful woman and when she got out of the limousine arrayed in white, one would have never suspected that she had ever been marred by a life of prostitution. She portrayed an air of child-like innocence, by the way she clung to her father's arm, while he escorted her down the aisle to give her away to the waiting groom.

Billy Joe and his best man waited together, dressed in white tuxedos with chests stuck out and chins raised as if they were elegant noblemen. Billy Joe's father, Reverend Cecil L. Williams, stood smiling politely, clutching the little black book which he would be reading the wedding vows out of.

Little Rodney, the ring bearer, stood stiff and straight, cradling two wedding bands, mounted on a white silk pillow. Charlotte, Nellie Mae's younger sister, and also a bridesmaid, was standing with the other bridesmaids and Sarah, who was the maid of honor. Both mothers, Billy Joe's and Nellie Mae's, wept quietly until the vows were over. Then, embraced the bride and groom and wished them

WARD STREET

happiness.

Charlotte had come up from Georgia with her father and mother for the wedding. She decided not to go back home when the wedding was over. Nellie Mae loved her sister, and took her to live with she and Billy Joe at Sarah's house. Sarah loved her too, and cared for Charlotte as her own.

Once again, God had filled her house with love and warmth...a family; Rodney, Charlotte, Billy Joe and Nellie Mae. The thought of becoming attached to loved ones again...family, and then losing them the way she had before, was more than Sarah cared to think about. She felt secure with everybody's relationship in the house but Rodney's. He had not been adopted yet.

Then came the day when Billy Joe and Nellie Mae were to visit the Department of Human Resources to try and make Rodney their own. Both, Billy Joe and Nellie Mae, were filled with anxiety when they stepped off the bus. They eagerly searched out the building where the Department of Human Resources was located. After they entered the building, they read a

WARD STREET

sign over a desk: 'INFORMATION.' They scurried over to the counter and were directed to where they could be seated in the waiting area.

Shortly, Billy Joe stood as they were approached by a young smiling colored woman. "Hello," she said. "My name is Linda. How can I help you?"

"We...we hope you can help us," Billy Joe stammered, reaching for Nellie Mae's hand. "I'm Billy Joe. This is my wife, Nellie Mae."

Nellie Mae took Billy Joe's hand and stood up. "We want to adopt a child," she told the social worker. "That's why we are here."

"Follow me," the social worker said.

They followed the young woman into her office, and seated themselves near her desk. The woman sat down, adjusted the typewriter and began typing. "You are married, of course. How long have you been married?"

"Three weeks," Nellie Mae beamed. "We are newly-weds."

"O-o-oh." the social worker commented. "The excitement hasn't worn off yet."

"We would like to think that we

WARD STREET

are still excited," Billy Joe said, squeezing Nellie Mae's hand. "We hope we will always be that way."

The social worker smiled. "It's possible. But you will have to work at it. Now, who do you want to adopt? Boy? Girl? Has the child already been chosen...someone you know? Or, had you planned to adopt a child from this agency?"

"It's someone we know," Nellie Mae told her. "A little three year old boy. We love him so much, we feel as if he belongs to us already."

"I, see. Your names again, please."

"Billy Joe and Nellie Mae williams," Billy Joe said.

"Are you employed, Mr. Williams?"

"Yes, we are both beauticians. We own a beauty shop."

"Now, this child that you want to adopt, are the parents alive?"

"Yes," Nellie Mae replied "But they won't cause any trouble. They are both drug addicts. They don't even care enough to take care of themselves, let alone a child. Little Rodney needs a home. Rodney...that's his name. Rodney Taylor."

WARD STREET

"What you are saying, Mrs. Williams, may be true. But still, we need the consent of the biological parents for the adoption. Of course, the courts will have to make the final decision after a thorough investigation has been made to determine if the child is being placed in a proper home.Ok? Well, Mr. and Mrs. Williams,We'll be getting in touch with you as soon as possible." She stood up and extended her hand to Billy Joe and Nellie Mae. "Thanks for coming in.There are lots and lots of lonely kids out there who need good fathers and mothers. I hope you two will be able to get the kid you want and give him a happy home. I will be praying for you."

Mr. Bud held the umbrella trying to shield everybody from the drizzle, as they climbed into his ol' cadillac. Little Rodney, his mother and the Puerto-Rican got into the front seat. Billy Joe, Nellie Mae and Agnes Taylor got into the back seat of the car.Mr. Bud slid behind the wheel and drove off to the courthouse.

Mr. Bud was a good man, and was always there in time of need. To-

WARD STREET

day was a special day for him. It was well known that most of Agnes Taylor's children were really his, including Rodney's mother. This made Rodney's adoption results very important to him.

They entered the courtroom, and Nellie Mae's heart raced with excitement! Yet, her soul was overwhelmed with anticipation and anxiety: 'what if she could not have Rodney? Suppose they won't let her have her son? What would she do? She loved this little boy so much. How could she live without him?'

Nellie Mae glanced over at Rodney being held by his mother and closed her eyes, gripping Billy Joe's arm for support. However, her neurosis was abandoned when she heard their case called to the bench.

When she and Billy Joe took their places before the judge, he paused for a moment, and squinted over the rim of his glasses, scrutinizing them carefully. "Mr. and Mrs. Williams...you are here to adopt one, Rodney Taylor, am I correct?"

"Yes, your Honor," Billy Joe answered.

WARD STREET

Nellie Mae nodded.

The judge turned to a young woman that Billy Joe and Nellie Mae recognized as the social worker they met when the adoption papers were filed. "Will the social worker representing this case come forward please?"

The woman approached the bench smiling at Billy Joe and Nellie Mae. "Your Honor, I have thoroughly investigated the Williamses, and I've found that they are a valued asset to the community. They are a hard working couple. In fact, they are in business for themselves. Also, I've learned that they are outstanding Church members. However, their past lives may be a bit questionable. During my investigation I found that Mr. Williams, for some reason, had a homosexual problem before he was married. And Mrs. Williams, is a former prostitute. Your Honor, despite the report, I believe the Williamses are completely reformed. I am sure that they will make good parents."

The judge did not hesitate to give his decision. "Perhaps the Williamses will make good parents, perhaps not. But there is no way that this court can turn this child over to a homosexual and a prostitute!"

"Ex,homosexual and prostitute," she emphasized."They have changed now."

"Ex,or whatever,"the judge persisted."There is no way that they are going to adopt this child!" The judge reclined into his chair and continued."Mr. and Mrs. Williams, maybe in the future, if, and when the laws are more lenient and the courts are not as particular, you will be able to adopt a child. But for the present..."

"Your Honor," Billy Joe interrupted, consoling Nellie Mae who was already in tears. "We need that boy, and he needs us. Rodney needs a home and we can give him one, and anything else he needs. Your Honor, you are holding our past against us...what we used to be. I will admit that we were wrong living the way we did. We have changed now. We wouldn't dare live that way again."

"Mr. Williams," the judge said sympathetically. "I believe you mean well. But I cannot take this responsibility upon myself, knowing what I already know about you. Now maybe; I'm not making any promises, now; but maybe, after you and Mrs. Williams have lived together for awhile as husband and wife, I may reconsider. But for now, there is nothing that I can do for you."

When they got out of the courthouse the rain had stopped, but nobody seemed to notice. The ride home was in silence and with mixed feelings: Billy Joe and Nellie Mae were devastated because they could not have Rodney for their own. Rodney's mother and the Puerto-Rican were disappointed because they did not want Rodney. Having to care for him meant another added responsibility which they could not afford.

Agnes Taylor pondered over the fact that, although she loved her grandson and wanted him for herself, she had no means to take care of him. She had raised thirteen children of her own, and it was not easy doing so. She was too old, and too tired to start raising children again, anyhow.

Mr. Bud loved his grandson, too, and wanted the very best for him.

WARD STREET

He knew that he was in an impossible situation. It would make his heart glad if Rodney could go home to live with him, but it would not be fair to his wife, Emma Jean. Mr. Bud always felt that Emma Jean had suspected him of having an affair with Agnes Taylor, although she never accused him. Emma Jean was a good, decent woman, and he loved her dearly. And he respected her. The relationship between him and Agnes existed only because his wife was a hopeless cripple.

Mr. Bud and Emma Jean had married when they were very young. Then, after just a few months of happiness together, Emma Jean was stricken with multiple sclerosis, followed by a series of strokes which left her an invalid. Realizing that she would never again function as a normal woman, and be the wife she knew her husband needed, she pleaded with Mr. Bud to leave her and be free. But he would not divorce her.

Over the years he paid for treatments by the best doctors, but Emma Jean never got any better than what she was. Refusing to put his wife into a nursing home,

WARD STREET

Mr. Bud took care of her himself, while he with a broken heart, watched her twisted body slowly deteriorate.

When the ol' caddy turned into Ward Street, even Rodney had not uttered a sound during the ride home from the courthouse. Sensing something was not quite right, he clung tenaciously to Nellie Mae, and kept his face buried in her bosom.

They got out of the car, and Nellie Mae attempted to put Rodney into his mother's arms, but he began to whimper. "You keep him, Nel," his mother said, withdrawing. "You are a much better mother than I could ever be, anyhow. Take him with you."

Nellie Mae started towards the house with Rodney in her arms. Then, turned back to his mother. "Thanks," she said. "Come see him when you want to."

The love for the child that Nellie Mae thought could never be fathered by Billy Joe was lavished upon Rodney. Nellie Mae labored long hours at the shop. She worked extra time, even after Billy Joe had gone home for the day, to buy what she wanted Rodney to have. Billy Joe loved Rodney, too. But he loved Nellie Mae even more, and the hours home without her were lonely hours.

Pure Unadulterated Innocence

Billy Joe soon found that he was sharing more of his life with Charlotte than with Nellie Mae. Nellie Mae had suggested, even insisted, that Charlotte keep Billy Joe and Rodney from being lonely while she was not there. The attachment between Billy Joe and Charlotte grew. Eventually, they were attracted physically.

Sarah, being as wise as she was, offered advice with a warning. "Be careful," she told them. "Both of you are two attractive people. You are spending too much time together. What's happening here is very apparent. It's dangerous. Billy Joe, this child is innocent. Compared to the life you have lived, she is a saint. Now, adultery is just as sinful as homosexuality. Both of those sins can send you straight to hell.I'm going to talk to both of you as if you were my own children. I'm sure there are many things about sex sins that you are not even aware of. You see, we hurt so many other than ourselves when we commit sex sins. Especially those closest to us. Be careful."

Sarah's words were heeded for awhile. But soon, Billy Joe and Charlotte found themselves drawn closer. Even into each other's arms.

It was Charlotte who attempted to break the enchantment. "No, Billy Joe," she insisted."This is all wrong. We can't hurt Nel, so. This is not right." She tried to retreat, but Billy Joe would not let her go.

Billy Joe, a man who had made love to both, women and men, and everything else in between, was more than a match for such pure innocence as Charlotte. He knew every trick in the book, and more besides. "Charlotte,have you ever had a man?Have you ever been made love to?"

Charlotte blushed...ashamed of what she felt. "No.I've never had a boy.Mamma and papa wouldn't let

WARD STREET

me...I mean, date anybody. They kept a close watch on me. Every time a boy would come to the house they would run him off. I suppose it was because of Nel. How it was with her when she left home...becoming a prostitute and all. I was surprised when mamma and papa didn't make me go back home after the wedding. Maybe they let me stay because I'm twenty one now."

Any guilt and remorse Charlotte had because Billy Joe was her sister's husband were shrugged off. She drew his arms even closer around her, and kissed him hard on the mouth. Charlotte's touch, the smell of her hair and the kiss, sent Billy Joe's senses off balance, and he was overwhelmed with guilt. Not only because he had been saved, and had given his heart to Jesus Christ; but because of Charlotte's innocence. He had never made love to anyone so innocent...a virgin. A remarkable contrast to the sex partners he was used to: the men, faggots, bi-sexuals, whores and prostitutes. And he was married to an ex-prostitute. She surely was not a virgin! Billy Joe suffered such condemnation when confronted with the possiblity of sinning against God, his wife, this young innocent person...and, oh yes, his own body until he feared disorder of the subconscious. Yet, any notions of piety that he felt were repudiated, and he entangled himself in a web of desire, ecstasy and sin!

What If?

The stench of smoldering hair intermingled with the cruel summer heat, had caused Nellie Mae to become frustrated and weak. It had also added intensely to the nausea and mounting discomfort she had already been experiencing for the past few days. She anxiously watched the clock, as she labored feebly over the head of hair she was working on. She kept casting frequent glances at those waiting in line.

Billy Joe suspected something was wrong. He had called the doctor earlier for an appointment.

Completely exhausted, Nellie Mae turned away from her work and flopped into a chair. "Billy Joe, I've had it. I'm going."

"Nel, you shouldn't be working in your condition, anyhow," Billy Joe told her. "I'll call a taxi for you. It's early but the doctor will see you if you're sick enough. I can take care of the shop myself."

Billy Joe helped Nellie Mae off with her smock, and dialed for a taxi. Within minutes, a taxi pulled up and stopped in front of the shop. Billy Joe put Nellie Mae into the back seat and kissed her good-bye.

"I feel terrible, Doc.," Nellie Mae said, when her turn came to see the doctor. I am sick at the stomach all the time. And I haven't seen my menstrual period in nearly six weeks. What could that be, Doc?"

"Sounds like a simple pregnancy to me." The doctor leaned back and laughed aloud! "Nothing to fret about. Getting pregnant is only normal."

Nellie Mae's mouth dropped open in disbelief. "Pregnant? Me? You must be kidding?"

"You just described the symptoms, perfectly."

"Couldn't there be some other condition that could cause all this?"

"I will have to run some tests."

"Please do."

"I'll get the nurse."

The doctor left the room, and in a few minutes a nurse appeared in the doorway. "Mrs. Williams, follow me, please."

Nellie Mae followed the nurse into one of the examining rooms and was told to strip. Her street clothes were replaced by only a gown with a split in the back. The nurse told her to lie on the table. She took Nellie Mae's pressure, told her that the doctor would be in to axamine her and left the room.

While lying on the table waiting for the doctor, Nellie Mae allowed her mind to run wild, pondering a multitude of questions: 'What if I am pregnant? What would it be? Boy? Girl? Smart? Stupid? Normal? Abnormal, Because of my sin as a prostitute? Bi-sexual, because of Billy Joe's homosexual tendencies? Maybe I should never have a child. If I am pregnant, I could have an abortion. No. That

WARD STREET

wouldn't be right. It would be murder!'

Foot steps were at the door, and the doctor came into the room and started examining her. "How are we doing Nellie?" the doctor teased. "let's see what we have here."

After a few amusing, "O-o-ohs, and a-a-ahs," the doctor gave her the results. "A heart-beat can be detected after six weeks, Nellie. And I've just discovered a health normal heart-beat. You are pregnant. Are you happy about it?"

Nellie Mae grew numb. She turned her face away from the doctor. 'What would she do now? What could she do?' Then, she gained the courage to except what she dreaded. "Well, Doc., I suppose that's that."

"You don't sound too enthusiastic."

"I just have to get used to the thought of God using me to bring another life into the world. My life will be different now. I will have to make some real adjustments."

"You can at least smile for us."

Nellie Mae managed a forced smiled. The doctor helped her sit up on the table, and told her to put her clothes on.

Before she left the office, all fear that her child might be abnormal left Nellie Mae, and she promised the doctor that with his help, she would take good care of herself.

The Deacons

Three months had gone by since the doctor's report had confirmed Nellie Mae's pregnancy. Billy Joe was proud of the fact that he was going to become a father. He felt good about himself, although he had many insults hurled at him from some who knew his past lifestyle.

Today was no different from any other day when he walked from work through his neighborhood. Many of the women, as he flaunted himself, embraced and kissed him, displaying unfeighed joy that Billy Joe was about to become a father. But, on the other hand, the men mocked him; bowing, taking off their hats, waving chivalrously. Billy Joe smiled and stuck out his chest even more in defiance against the insults, slurs and degrading remarks.

"Here comes the madam," they jeered. "Madam Billy Joe!"

"You think you are a man now, don't you? You faggot, you!"

"Hey, Billy Joe! Who's going to have that baby...you or Nellie Mae?"

"Pervert!"

"Faggot!"

Soon, Billy Joe was through the stigma, and near his own house. Rodney ran to meet him when he got closer. "Billy Joe! Billy Joe! Hey, Billy Joe!"

Billy Joe prepared himself, and caught Rodney as he leaped into his arms. "Hi, ol' buddie. How've you been doing today?"

"Billy Joe, somebody's in the house waiting to see you!"

"To see, me? Who? I wonder."

"From the Church. Deacons, I think."

"Oh, they are probably here to see aunt Sarah."

Both Deacons stood when Billy Joe came through the doorway with Rodney in his arms.

Sarah sat smiling.

"Hello, Billy Joe," one of the

WARD STREET

Deacons greeted, extending his hand. "How are, you?"

Billy Joe stood Rodney on the floor and took the Deacon's hand. "I'm fine, Deacon Wilson. How are, you? It's good to see you." he turned his attention to the other Deacon and took his hand. "Deacon Sanders, how are, you? What are you doing in our neck of the woods this evening?"

"How are, you, Billy Joe? Well, the Chairman, here, asked me to come over with him on a little business. You see..."

"Sit down," Billy Joe gestured. Everybody sat down, and Deacon Sanders continued. "Billy Joe, we are in need of Deacons at the Church. So, my Chairman, here, asked me to come with him to talk to you about coming on the Deacon Board."

"Amen," Deacon Wilson agreed. "Billy Joe, we only have a few Deacons now. Many of our Deacons have died, and the few we have are old, and can't serve that well anymore. Now you are a young man. We need men like you."

Billy Joe blushed and glanced at Sarah.

"You have to make up your own

mind," Sarah said. "I can't do that for you."

"Billy Joe," Deacon Wilson said. "We know all about your past life. Deacon Sanders, myself, and the rest of the board have already talked it over with your father, the Reverend. We all believe that you are a good man." The Deacon laughed apologetically. He continued slyly. "Me and my Co-Chairman, we've been checking on you now." He laughed again.

"W-well, r-right now," Billy Joe stammered. "My wife is pregnant, and..."

"That's something in your favor," Deacon Wilson interrupted. "We want family men...men who know how to rule their own house well." Deacon Wilson shifted his attention to Sarah, who was already thumbing through her Bible. "Sister Sarah, read, First Timothy, chapter three, verses four through thirteen."

"Amen," Sarah said, after flipping a few more pages. "And it reads as follows: **One that ruleth well his own house, having his children in subjection with all gravity;**

For if a man know not how to

rule his own house, how shall he take care of the church of God?

Not a novice, lest being lifted up with pride he fall into the condemnation of the devil.

Moreover he must have a good report of them which are without; lest he fall into reproach and the snare of the devil.

Likewise must the deacons be grave, not double tongued, not given to much wine, not greedy of filthy lucre;

Holding the mystery of the faith in a pure conscience.

And let these also first be proved; then let them use the office of a deacon, being found blameless.

Even so must their wives be grave, not slanderers, sober, faithful in all things.

Let the deacons be the husbands of one wife, ruling their children and their own houses well.

For they that have used the office of a deacon well purchase to themselves a good degree, and great boldness in the faith which is in Christ Jesus."
I Timothy 3:4-13.

"Amen," Deacon Wilson continued, when Sarah finished reading.

WARD STREET

"Praise The Lord! Do you understand the Scripture sister Sarah just read, Billy Joe? See what it says about the wife there in verse eleven? It says: 'even so must their wives be grave, not slanderers, sober, faithful in all things.' This means we need your wife, too. A man needs a good wife when he's on the Deacon Board. Soon as your wife has had her baby, she can come on the Board as a Deaconess and join you..." he laughed and added..."anymore excuses?"

Sarah closed the Bible and laid it on the table. "Billy Joe," she said. "The reason the Church is asking you and Nel to come on the Board, they believe you to be good people. Since you and Nel have been living here with me, you and she have proven to be just that. I love both of you as if you were my own dear children. Now that you have the baby coming, that really put the icing on the cake. I have been praying for both of you for a long time. It looks as if God has answered my prayers."

Deacon Wilson stood up. "Billy Joe, we should be talking to your wife, too. Is she here?"

WARD STREET

Billy Joe looked at Sarah.

"She's upstairs," Sarah said. "Rodney, get Nel for us."

Rodney dashed up the stair steps, and in a few minutes Nellie Mae came down rubbing her eyes sleepishly. "Hello, everybody. I didn't know we had company."

"Hi, Nellie," Deacon Wilson said, reaching for her hand. "Sorry, we had to wake you."

Deacon Sanders stood up smiling. "Nel, how are, you?"

"Fine, thank you." she smiled back at him and sat down.

The Deacons remained standing.

"What's the purpose of this occasion?" Nellie Mae wanted to know. "Something special going on that I don't know about?"

"We are here to talk to you and your husband concerning the Deacon and Deaconess Board," Deacon Wilson told her. "We believe that you and Billy Joe are needed on the board."

Nellie Mae blinked her eyes, flabbergasted. "Deacon and Deaconess Board? Me? Us? We don't deserve this, do we?"

"Don't be surprised," Deacon Sanders said. "None of us were always saints. I was not always a

WARD STREET

saint."

"Oh, I know you were not always a saint, Deacon," Nellie Mae laughed. I knew you long before you joined the Church."

Deacon Sanders obviously embarrassed, shifted from one uncomfortable postion to another. He did manage to chuckle a bit when everybody else started laughing. "I wasn't all that bad, now," he said. "I just loved sinning like everybody else."

"You loved it alright, Deacon," Nellie Mae agreed. "You have had your fun."

After everyone had quieted down, Deacon Wilson gathered everybody in a circle for prayer. "Billy Joe," he said. "You are now what we call a walking Deacon. We'll give you six months to walk and prove yourself. You and Nellie Mae will make out alright. Both of you will need time to prepare yourselves. Prayer and Bible study are needed. You need to know the Word. Study to show yourselves approved. Get acquainted with God through His Word. Know His Ways. Learn to love and obey Him. We're going to pray and ask God to help us, right now. Let us pray."

WARD STREET

The Deacons prayed and left, leaving Billy Joe and Nellie Mae to study and prepare themselves for the service of God.

Sarah closed the door behind the Deacons. Then, turned her attention to Billy Joe and Nellie Mae."I want to talk to you.I have put it off long enough. There is something very important that we need to talk about. Nellie Mae, your sister is pregnant, too."

The blood drained out of Nellie Mae's face, and she seemed faint. "Charlotte...pregnant?This...this can't be real.This just can't be. Are you sure, aunt Sarah? Are you sure?"

"According to her doctor, her baby is due same time as yours. Nellie, Charlotte wanted to tell you herself but she couldn't, so she asked me to do it.She is very upset."

"I imagine she is upset,"Nellie Mae said."She just made her journey through this life even more complicated, by adding extra baggage. I ran the street for years, but I never got myself pregnant. It's hard for me to accept this. What will I tell mamma and papa? They are going to blame me, for this."

Billy Joe moved about the room uneasily, eyeing Nellie Mae, trying to avoid suspicion. "Are you sure she's pregnant, aunt Sarah? She looks alright to me."

"Naturally, you would never detect something like that as quickly as I would, Billy Joe," Sarah told him. "You are a man. A woman will notice certain things about another woman that a man just wouldn't pay any attention to. I've known for some time now that Charlotte was pregnant. I just wouldn't say anything. She wore full cut clothes but she was not able to hide something like that from me. I knew."

Nellie Mae held Rodney tightly in her lap. She clung to him as if she were afraid she would lose him. As if he were her only security, now. "Aunt Sarah, how could she possibly be pregnant? All she does is go to work. She's not dating anybody. Maybe it's somebody she works with."

"Whoever it is," Sarah said hopefully. "I pray it's somebody she will be able to marry. I hate to see any young woman mess up her life by having a child out of wedlock, and Charlotte is such a lovely person. She's so innocent. I feel as if she's my own daughter."

"Yeah," Billy Joe muffled. "She's a good kid alright." He made an excuse and left the room.

Sarah, Nellie Mae and Rodney were still there in the living room when Charlotte got home from work. Rodney scrambled out of Nellie Mae's lap, sprinted towards Charlotte when she came through the doorway, and vaulted into her arms. "Here's Charlotte! Here's Charlotte! Hey, everybody, Charlotte's home!"

"Hi, sweetheart," Charlotte said, kissing Rodney after securing him in her arms. "Glad to see me, huh?"

Rodney gripped Charlotte tightly around the neck. "Glad to see you!"

"Charlotte," Nellie Mae began. "Why did you do this to me? To us? To yourself? What happened? Who did this?"

Charlotte immediately subdued her emotions. She stood Rodney on the floor, sat down and kept quiet.

"Say something to me!" Nellie Mae shouted. "You are pregnant! Say something!"

WARD STREET

Charlotte spoke very quietly. She stared into space as if she were in a trance. "Yes, I am pregnant, Nel. For weeks, I've wanted to tell you but I couldn't. It hurts so much. I-I've hurt everybody. Everybody will have to forgive me. I have hurt everybody, so. Mamma and papa will have to forgive me. I'm sure God will forgive me. And if I don't forgive myself, I will not be able to live with myself."

"Charlotte," Nellie Mae said. "I suppose I am part blame for this. When mamma and papa left you up here with me, I should have talked to you about dating. And sex. I never mentioned men, because at your age, I was sure that you could take care of yourself. Who did this? Who was the man?"

Charlotte blushed. She got up from where she was sitting, and moved over to the stair case and stood. "A boy," she said quietly. "A boy."

***

WARD STREET

CHAPTER-10

THE ORDINATION
Two daughters

It was Sunday evening, and the Church was crowded with scarely standing room.The Ordination Sermon Preached, the offering taken, and one of the visiting Deacons prayed over the offering. Then, just when another Deacon stood to present the Hymn Book, a note was pasted up to the Pulpit for the Pastor.

Reverend Williams read the note and stood up. He strode to the desk and addressed the crowd. "I have just been informed that my son, here, has just become the proud father of a nine pound, two ounce baby girl! Which means, I have just become a brand new grandaddy! Stand up Billy Joe!Let the folks see who you are. We are proud of you!"

Awkwardly,Billy Joe stood while everyone cheered.

"Praise The, Lord!" The Pastor continued."Praise The,Lord! Billy Joe is a brand new daddy, now! Go on son..." he motioned to the

WARD STREET

Deacon who had the Hymn Book,... "finish what you started."

The Deacon cleared his throat and composed himself as he stood before Billy Joe and two other young men being Ordained. "The Word says that you are to be filled with the Spirit, speaking to yourselves in Psalms and Hymns and Spiritual songs, singing and making melody in your hearts to The Lord. Now this Hymn Book, will help you do just that. You may not be able to sing like Paul and Silas, who sang and prayed so mightily there in prison 'til they started an earth quake, shaking the jail in such a way, the jailor fell down before them and cried, 'What must I do to be saved?' Perhaps you will never be able to sing like that, but you can sing something. In fact, you may have hardly any singing voice at all. Or, you may sing off key; or you may be unable to carry a tune. But my God can take the most unskilled voice there is, that is truly committed to Him and saturate it with His Holy Spirit, and shape, and reshape the entire world. So I am presenting to you this Hymn Book; take the Book, memorize as many of these great Hymns of the Church as you can. Worship God with your singing and you will find that you will always receive a blessing. Thank you, and may God bless you!" He handed each of the candidates a Hymn Book and sat down.

Reverend Williams got up again and stood at the desk. His eyes swept the congregation, searching the crowd. "Well, we'll call on another one of our visiting Deacons to present the Bible; this young man right here...stand up son, tell folks who you are."

"Rodgers," the man said, getting up from where he was, smiling. "Deacon Edward Rodgers. Pilgrim, Baptist Church." He stepped forward with the Bible, and stood sway-backed before the three men, and squared his shoulders. "This Book, we call the Bible, is the Book of books. Now, if you want this Book to work for you, you have to read it. Not only do you have to read this Book, you have to apply it to your life. When Satan comes against you...take note now, it is not 'if' he comes against you...it's 'when!' Oh, yes, he will surely come against you,

WARD STREET

now that you are a Deacon and are being Ordained into the service of The Lord. When"...

"Amen, Deacon," from the congregation.

"Say so!'

..."When the Devil comes against you with all the power that he can muster from hell itself, this Book will sustain you. It is your weapon! Now, the Bible says that we are to put on the whole armor of God, that we may be able to stand against the wiles of the Devil. For..."

"Oh, yes! Yes, yes, Deacon," somebody encouraged. "Tell it like it is!"

The Deacon stabilized his composure and proceeded. "For we wrestle not against flesh and blood, but against principalities, against powers, against the rulers of the darkness of this world, against spiritual wickedness in high places..."

"That's the truth, Deacon," more encouragement. "Say on."

"Hallelujah!"

"Amen!"

"Praise The Lord!"

"C'mon, Deacon!" Reverend Williams exclaimed. "Tell it!"

WARD STREET

Deacon Rodgers secured his posture, and continued. "When you read this Book, you will be putting on the whole armor of God, and will be able to stand in the evil day"...

"Oh, yes!"

..."This Book can be used as your breastplate of righteousness; with it your feet will be shod with the preparation of the gospel of peace; it is your shield of faith, wherewith you shall be able to quench all the fiery darts of the wicked"...

"Amen!"

..."This Word here, is your helmet of salvation, and the Sword of the Spirit, which is the Word of God! In this Book, you will find food when you're hungry,...Spiritual food that is; comfort when you need comforting; friend and companionship if you're lonely." The Deacon handed each of the men a Bible. "Now, gentlemen, this is your Sword, use it skillfully, for you will have to, now that you have become a Deacon. Satan will come against you now more than ever! Read the Book of Acts, the sixth and seventh chapters. You will find there, the account of

WARD STREET

Stephen, one of the first Ordained Deacons of the Church. Stephen was a man of faith, and he Preached the Word with such power, he was stoned to death. Now, you may never have to die for the sake of the gospel, but when Satan gets done with you, you will know that you have been in a good fight. Take this Book, read and study it daily, and apply it to your life. It is the only way you will ever be able to stand against all the fiery darts that the Devil will be hurling at you. Thank you, and God bless you!" The Deacon went back to where he was sitting, while the congregation applauded.

Reverend Williams got up and leaned over the desk. "Well done, Deacon," he said. "Thank you. Job well done." He came down from the Pulpit, followed by the guest and associated Ministers. "Well, brethren, let's lay hands on these young brethren, here. And pray for them. C'mon, c'mon you Deacons. Let us make a big strong line, here. We are going to ask our Chairman, to do the praying. C'mon, over here, Deacon Wilson, and pray for these young men."

Deacon Wilson, smiling politely

WARD STREET

as usual, moved gracefully into the midst of the Ministers and Deacons, as they began laying hands on the three candidates.

Deacon Wilson was a good man, who loved God, and it reflected in his praying. It was said, that when he prayed, his great booming voice could be heard over much of the neighborhood. When his voice was heard through the streets, even the prostitutes and the drug addicts paid attention. It was rumored that the wineos kept the caps of their wine bottles in place until he finished praying.

Deacon Wilson prayed with tears streaming down both cheeks, and lapping under his chin. Whenever he would reach a high point in his prayer, trying to convince God of an immediate need, his voice would quiver. It was said that, "If there was anybody that could reach the Heart of God, Deacon Wilson could do it."

After the prayer, the Charge was given to the three candidates by Deacon Sanders, the Co-Chairman, and everybody went home.

When Billy Joe, Sarah and Rodney got home from Church, they

met Charlotte at the door, struggling with a heavy suit case. "I'm on my way to the hospital to have my baby," she told them. "I have been having birth pangs all day. They are coming closer, now. I could have my baby at any moment." Charlotte started crying, and Rodney tugged urgently at her skirt. "Charlotte, are you sick? Are you real sick?"

"Yes, I am," she said. She managed a faint smile, but staggered against Rodney. "And a little weak."

Sarah steadied Charlotte in her arms, and Billy Joe took her bag.

"How are you going to the hospital, child?" Sarah wanted to know. "Did you call a taxi, yet?"

"No, I didn't call a taxi. I was on my way to the bus stop."

"Bus stop? You don't have no time for that! Billy Joe, get Mr. Bud. He'll take us. We were going to the hospital to see Nellie Mae, anyhow. It would have been better had you and Nel gone to the hospital together."

"Is Nel sick, too?" Rodney questioned earnestly.

"Yes, Nel's sick, too," Sarah laughed, cradling his head against her thigh. "Both of our girls are sick today. We'll be able to see Nel in a few minutes."

Mr. Bud pulled to the curb, and Billy Joe bailed out on the pavement. He scurried over and met Charlotte, put his arm around her, picked up the suit case and took her over to the car. Billy Joe put Charlotte and the suit case into the back seat, along with Sarah and Rodney, then slid into the seat with Mr. Bud.

Several minutes from the house, Sarah urged Mr. Bud to pull over to the curb. Charlotte's baby was coming already!

Soon, with the help of Mr. Bud and Billy Joe, and Rodney's encouragement, Sarah was holding a beautiful little baby girl wrapped in her shawl, and Mr. Bud headed towards the hospital again.

When they got to the hospital, Billy Joe ran in and brought out a doctor and two nurses. The umbilical cord was cut, and Charlotte, with her new baby girl was carried into the hospital and cared for.

While Sarah made certain that Charlotte and the baby were secure, Billy Joe went to join Nellie Mae.

Although the deep shadows under her eyes bore evidence of strain and fatigue, Nellie Mae was able to smile and extend her arms, when Billy Joe appeared in the doorway of her room."We have a sweet little baby daughter,"she told Billy Joe. "She's beautiful."

Billy Joe took Nellie Mae in his arms and kissed her. "I know, I know," he said. "And I love the two of you, so much. I can barely wait to see our little daughter."

"Go and see her," Nellie Mae said."She's down in the nursery."

Nellie Mae released Billy Joe from her arms, and when he got to the doorway, he stopped. "Your sister had her baby a few minutes ago. She's right here in the hospital.She had a little girl,too."

Nellie Mae's eyes lit up."Really? I know she's beautiful!"

"She is beautiful.Charlotte had her baby in the car, before we could get her to the hospital."

"O-o-oh, no! Is she alright?"

"She's fine, as far as I know. I'm going to check on her after I go and see our little Nellie."

"Rachel," Nellie Mae said softly, cradling her lips in her fingers. "I want to call our baby, Rachel, if it's alright with you."

"Well, whatever. It doesn't really matter what we call her if she is as pretty as you are." Billy Joe winked at Nellie Mae and disappeared through the doorway. He took the elevator down to the floor where the nursery was.

When he approached the glass enclosure where the newborns were kept, he fastened his eyes upon the little blue eyed baby girl being held near the window by a middle-aged blond nurse. "Can I help, you?" the nurse asked.

"I came to see my little daughter," Billy Joe replied, staring at the baby she held.

"What?" the nurse exclaimed, wide-eyed. "What's her name?"

"Rachel."

"O-o-oh, that one," she sighed in relief. "I'll get her for you." She put the baby she was holding in her crib, and brought Rachel to the window. "Beautiful, isn't she?"

"Yes," Billy Joe said. "She is beautiful. Wish I could touch her."

"You may, later. Meanwhile, she's in my care...right, precious?"

WARD STREET

She smiled at Rachel and took her back to her crib.

Billy Joe reluctantly left the nursery and Rachel, and went to Charlotte's room.

Charlotte was alone when Billy Joe came into the room. She was asleep but when he came near the bed, she woke up. "O-o-oh, Billy Joe, Billy Joe. This is a terrible thing we've done. I don't see how we could ever forgive ourselves. Nel won't forgive us, either. She is sure to learn the truth. Something as obvious as this just can't be kept a secret. She will know. She will know."

When Billy Joe came into the room, he had moved a chair near the bed, and he sat drooped as if a heavy burden was upon him. Guilt and sorrow were so dominant, his entire form...his physique, seemed drawn out of proportion; even smaller, as if he were trying to pull himself into a shell. When he began to speak his voice was hollow and weak, as if he had lost all hope. "Charlotte, I love Nel so much it's hell to even think of ever losing her. Nellie Mae took me out of a confused life of misery and sin, and taught me how

WARD STREET

to express myself as a man. I lived the life of a homosexual for so long, I lost my true identity. Nellie Mae is responsible for me discovering my manhood. Before she came along and convinced me that I didn't have to live the way that I was living, I was nothing. Now, I am a husband and a father. What I've done...what we have done, cannot be undone, and it is going to destroy me."

The nurse came into the room and placed Charlotte's baby in her arms. She made Charlotte and the baby as comfortable as she could. "I have cleaned her up for you," she said. "All eight pound three ounces of her. She is the cutest little thing in this hospital. What are you going to name her?"

"Charlotte." Charlotte forced a faint smile. "I'm going to name my baby, Charlotte. I'm giving her my own name. My mother's name is Charlotte, too."

"Oh, that's a beautiful name," the nurse turned her attention to Billy Joe, "don't you think so, sir? Are you the lucky father?"

"No, I am her uncle. Charlotte is my wife's sister."

WARD STREET

"Well, better luck next time." The nurse left the room.

Charlotte moved her head from side to side, despairingly. She clutched the baby in her arms,and held her tightly to her bosom. "Billy Joe, this is our baby.This our baby, and nothing can ever change that. Nothing!"

Billy Joe leaned over and looked at little Charlotte closely. "Yes,she's our baby.And she looks just like Rachel. They could almost pass for twins,and they look just like me.Nel will know.Everybody will know!"

Suddenly,Sarah was in the room, excited!"Charlotte,you should see Nel's baby! She is beautiful!O-o-oh, you've got your baby,now. Let me see her. Isn't she nice. She looks just like Rachel. They are both beautiful babies. Oh, won't Nel be surprised when she see this baby. Isn't it remarkable... the resemblance and all?"

"Yes,it is remarkable,Billy Joe said, trying not to act suspicious. "It's all in the family, aunt Sarah." He managed to chuckle.

"Billy Joe, we left Mr. Bud and Rodney in the car," Sarah said.

WARD STREET

"I'm sure they have gotten impatient by now. We had better be going."

"I'll go see Nel again before I go," Billy Joe said, and left the room.

During the ride home, everybody was full of chatter. Mr. Bud and Rodney asking questions about the babies. Sarah and Billy Joe supplying the answers.

The night had nearly slipped away into early dawn, as Billy Joe lay considering the events that had occurred over the past twenty four hours. The enthusiasm he felt because of the Ordination, plus the ecstasy and apprehension he was experiencing because of becoming a father twice in the same day, one legitimate and one not, had robbed him of sleep. He was filled with joy and excitement over the legitimate child Nellie Mae had borne him, because it was an expression of his manhood, confirming his heterosexuality. On the other hand, joy and excitement were opposed by guilt and fear, because of the illegitimate child Charlotte had borne.

WARD STREET

Billy Joe agonized because he was guilt ridden for what he had done. He had allowed sensuality, a few moments of sexual pleasure to take precedence over his life again. Before, when he permitted sex to rule his life, it was through homosexuality. But God had saved him, and taken him out of that sin. Now, this sin of adultery seemed worse, because it involved so many innocent people so dear to him. Finally, he did fall asleep, but restless sleep, disturbed by haunting dreams of his two daughters.

In the dream, he was back at the hospital standing at the window of the nursery room. The same blond nurse was standing at the window smiling. Now, she was holding both babies; Rachel and charlotte.

The infants looked exactly alike. Both, with Billy Joe's head and likeness on their torso, and what magnified the apprehension, the nurse extending the infants for Billy Joe to receive, but when he reached out to take them, he was evaded. The greater the effort to reach the nurse and the infants, the more evasive they became. Then, they disappeared into an endless vacuum, and Billy Joe collapsed exhausted to the floor.

The jolt brought Billy Joe out of bed and onto his feet. Staring out the window into the early morning sunrise, he collected his thoughts and laid down again. He was now wide awake, pondering the unprofitable circumstances that he alone was responsible for.

Confession

Sarah sat at the kitchen table and sipped a cup of coffee. She listened quietly while Billy Joe poured out his troublesome heart. He was confessing to Sarah, relying on her strength. "Aunt Sarah, you are truly a lady of wisdom. You saw all this coming before it actually happened. You warned us. You tried to help us, then. Help us, now. Please, show us what to do. We need you now, more than ever."

"Billy Joe, I feel as guilty as you feel, because I was not persistent enough. Nellie Mae will be hurt the most here. You are her husband. How will you face Nel with something like this?"

"Aunt Sarah, I was hoping that maybe you could help me out... could...perhaps, tell her for me. You always seem to be able to say the right words and all. Would you?"

"Billy Joe, this is something you will have to do yourself. You got yourself into this mess, you will have to get yourself out of it. I am more than willing to help you with anything else, but this you will have to do."

"Pray for me, aunt Sarah. At least, pray for me."

Sarah prayed for Billy Joe. Then, she was left alone. Alone to ponder her own guilt, although it was needless now to accept or repudiate blame. The dreadful results of the sinful relationship between these two people had already manifested. Everyone would suffer now because of their carelessness.

Nellie Mae paused in the doorway, leaning against the door frame before disturbing Charlotte and the baby. Both, were sleeping

WARD STREET

peacefully. Nellie Mae had left her room for the first time since she had been in the hospital. She wanted To talk to Charlotte, and see her baby.

Charlotte opened her eyes sluggishly when Nellie Mae sat on the side of the bed, admiring little Charlotte. She turned her head to avoid Nellie Mae's eyes. "Oh, Nel, Nel...I'm so ashamed!"

"No, no, now. Don't be too hard on yourself. What's done, is done. You have to go on living, despite of what has happened. Nothing will be changed by worrying. You can raise your daughter without being married. You are not alone. You will always have me. We will always be together; you and me, Billy Joe, Rachel and little Charlotte."

Charlotte threw herself into Nellie Mae's arms, and Nellie Mae held her close. "Oh, Nel," Charlotte cried. "Billy Joe is little Charlotte's father, too! Forgive, me! Forgive, me! I know I have hurt you! I have hurt you!"

Nellie Mae, because of the sudden shock, was grieved beyond measure. Realizing this pitiful situation, her heart broke. She gathered Charlotte closer to her breast,and rocked her to and fro.

Both, Charlotte and Nellie Mae, moaned, groaned, and lamented aloud! Unrestrainedly!

Charlotte wept for the hurt and misery she had brought upon the three people on this earth that she loved the most;her mother,her father, and Nellie mae. She wept so for her parents because they had been so careful to keep her pure. She was raised in a Christian home, and had been taught to live a life apart from fornication. They had trained her well. She had lived a life of abstinence! She loved her parents. Yet, she had disappointed both of them.

Then, there was Nellie Mae. Her only beloved sister. Nellie Mae loved her, and took her into her own home to live with her and Billy Joe.It was her own sister's husband with whom she had committed this horrible sin.'Oh,why had she allowed herself to become so careless? She undoubtedly, knew better. She was a responsible person. She could not excuse herself.'

Nellie Mae not only felt sorrow

for Charlotte, but for her own life. Her entire world had just come crashing down. She and Billy Joe had just come out of a life of sexual perversion. They had accepted each other the way they were, and had gotten married. They had become united as husband and wife with the hopes, that a better life could be built for both of them. There was also the understanding that the marriage was supported on the fact that according to how they had lived before, being married to each other could not be worse. Now, this! Things had gotten worse.

The phone had stopped ringing, and Nellie Mae could hear Rodney's voice on the other end of the line. "Hello."
"Rodney?"
"Hey! This is Nel!"
"Rodney. Hi, honey. Let me speak to aunt Sarah."
Nellie Mae heard Rodney yelling for Sarah. Within a few seconds, she was on the line. "Nellie Mae, how are you, dear?"
"Well, I'm alright."
"You may be alright, Nel, but you sound so tired."

WARD STREET

"I am tired, aunt Sarah. I am worried and depressed."

"Anything I can do?"

"What I need most of all, aunt Sarah, is for someone to pick us up from the hospital."

"Good. I'll get Billy Joe..."

"No, aunt Sarah, don't bother getting Billy Joe. Just tell him something for me. Tell him..." Nellie Mae wept, then continued, "...not to be there when I get there."

"Then you know..."

"About him and Charlotte? Yes."

"Why don't you and Billy Joe talk first before you decide on anything. The relationship between you and him might still be saved. Who knows?"

"There's nothing for him and me to talk about, aunt Sarah. I have already made my decision. He made his decision when he made love to my sister. Billy Joe has hurt me, aunt Sarah. He has hurt me."

Sarah consoled Nellie Mae the best she could, then told her that she would send Mr. Bud to pick up her, Charlotte and the babies.

***

WARD STREET

CHAPTER-11

THE DOG RETURNS TO ITS VOMIT
You Can Be Sure Your Sin Will Find You Out

For the past few months, Billy Joe had been living in a state of woe. Everything that he had ever cared about was lost...shattered! His wife and baby; his new way of life...gone!

Sin, had also relieved him of his duties as a Deacon. Billy Joe was terminated before he ever got a chance to serve. The shortest known service in Church history!

Concerning Billy Joe and his sin, it was his mother who suffered the most. When he was ousted out of office because of adultery, it opened old wounds in his mother's heart that were there because of his former life-style, as a homosexual. It brought to mind the pain and disappointment she experienced when she first discovered that her precious son was gay. She had never quite gotten over the impact that muddled her conception when she had come home unexpectedly and entered her

WARD STREET

bedroom, only to find her Billy Joe admiring himself in the mirror, dressed in her clothes, from panties to makeup. When she questioned, why? He had admitted that he was gay, without any regret.

She suffered immeasurably, but the wounds were healed when Billy Joe repented of his terrible sin, got married and fathered a child. Now, her heart was bleeding again. Billy Joe loved his mother dearly and lamented with her, although whatever he did now would never change anything. His mother was more transparent than his father, so therefore, her suffering was more visible. It was obvious that his mother was miserable, but he was also aware that his father had become disillusioned.

Billy Joe felt that if he could only get Nellie Mae to talk to him, he could dissuade the condemnation and contempt she had for him. She agreed to talk to him but only on the phone. He pleaded with her for reconciliation, but to no avail.

"No, Billy Joe, I loved you, but everything that I ever felt for you is gone now. I am not so proud that I could not have forgiven you for having an affair with another woman, but you chose my own sister. I suppose I will have to forgive you for the sake of all that is Holy, but I can never live with you as your wife again. I loved you Billy Joe because you and I were so much alike. God brought us from a long ways. He took both of us out of a life of sexual perversion and gave us another chance at life. I'm grateful myself. You should be, too."

"Nel, I am grateful. I thank God everyday for what He has done for me. God gave me a wife and a child. He made my life worth living. If I lose you and Rachel, I will be just like I was before. I will have nothing worth living for. I know what I did was wrong, in fact, it's taking all that I can do, just to ask you to forgive me. I need you, Nel. You are my strength. I won't be able to make it on my own. I am a weak man. Help me...!"

"Billy Joe, you are out of my life, and I have sent Charlotte back home. I hated to put all this burden on mamma and papa, but I had to get Charlotte out of my house. I still love Charlotte, but it was not good having her in the same house with me."

"Nel, what are we going to do about our business...the shop?"

"You run the business. Take the shop. It's yours. I'm already working somewhere else. If it weren't for the baby, I wouldn't have any dealings with you at all. It's only fair that you see Rachel sometime. You do have visiting rights. You have to support her, too."

"I will support her, Nel...both of you."

"No, not me. Rachel. I will take care of myself. The less I see of you, the better off I will be."

There was a click when Nellie Mae hung up. That click, turned Billy Joe's life off. From that moment on, he was in a state of irrevocable depression. In the weeks that followed, he was back into the same old life-style.

He stopped going to Church, and started hanging out with the same old crowd again. The gays. Hours at the shop became abnormal; late openings and early closings. Most times Billy Joe did not bother to open at all. Near the end, most of

WARD STREET

his clientele were gays and lesbians anyhow. Finally, the shop was closed for good.

Agnes Taylor, Emma Jean And Mr. Bud

The brisk morning air on Ward street was suddenly broken by sharp piercing shrieks, as Agnes Taylor ran wildly in the street screaming! Her skirt was raised above her waistline. She ran to every man in the street, gyrating, and jerking her naked buttock. A crowd had gathered, and some cheered, while others jeered, and made sport.

Sarah caught a glimpse of the pathetic scene from her window, and it broke her heart to see Agnes in such a pitiful condition. She had predicted that Miss Agnes would someday go mad because of her depraved notions toward sex. Sarah went out into the street where Agnes was, and tried to bring her under control. Agnes let go of her skirt just long enough to frail franticly at Sarah, with both hands flying, ripping and

WARD STREET

tearing until Sarah was almost naked herself. Realizing that she was no match for Agnes in her present state, Sarah retreated back into the house for safety.

Mr. Bud and Emma Jean heard the commotion from the second floor of their house. Mr. Bud drew back the curtain of the bedroom window to see what was going on. He unmistakably recognized Agnes in the crowd even though she had her back towards him. When the crowd shifted and he could see that she was naked, he hurried down into the street where she was.

Agnes was a beautiful woman, and although she had aged, her natural beauty was still evident. The graying hair, broken lines and wrinkles had failed to conceal the essence of what she was. The straight hair and high cheek bones, clearly revealed that the blood running in her veins was more Algonkian Indian, than African American Negro.

The skirt Agnes was wearing had been completely torn off now, and the lower portion of her torso was exposed to the spectators. Some of the lewd men and drunks tried to take advantage of her, but when Mr. Bud pushed his way through the crowd, the men recognized who he was. They respectfully moved out of his way. Agnes was aware of his presence, too. She lowered her head with guilt. She was ashamed, and subdued herself. Mr. Bud took off his coat and covered her as best as he could. The crowd began to break up. Finally, though unwillingly, everyone left. Mr. Bud and Agnes were left alone, crying in each others arms.

When her husband had bounded down the stairs to the commotion in the street, Emma Jean had struggled to pull her crippled body up in the bed, and to a proper position where she could see out of the window. In her almost futile effort to reach the window, she missed most of what was going on. She did see enough to cause her to feel sorry for Agnes Taylor, and witness the authority and gentleness which her husband used to bring everything under control.

Mr. Bud and Agnes Taylor stood clinging to each other with kisses and tears mingling, as if the rest of the world had been shut

WARD STREET

out...forgotten! What Emma Jean saw from the window, confirmed what she had known all those years, but would not accept as truth, that Agnes Taylor and her husband were lovers.

Emma Jean watched until the embrace was broken, and Mr. Bud started leading Agnes towards the house. 'Our house,' she thought. 'Why is Buddy bringing that woman to our house?' Tearfully, Emma Jean withdrew from the window, and eased back upon her pillow. 'Well, I'm sure she needs him now more than I do.'

She heard Mr. Bud trudging up the stairway with Agnes Taylor. Then, they were standing in the doorway of her bedroom, as if undecided what they should do next.

When Emma Jean first heard Agnes Taylor's foot steps on the stairway, there was no doubt in her mind, that when she saw this woman face to face, she would have nothing in her heart but hatred and rejection for her. But what she saw in the doorway, broke her heart instead. This poor miserable, pitiful creature whom she wanted so desperately to hate, needed to be cared for. She realized that ultimately, she had come face to face with someone more crippled than herself.

Emma Jean, sensing Agnes Taylor's urgent need, reached out to her in love, extending her shriveled arms as far as she could, wincing and grimacing in unsuccessful attempts to raise herself off the pillow. Agnes Taylor, reading the earnest expressions on Emma Jean's face, moved over to where she was, and gently unraveled her slender warped arms and placed them around her own body, and these two women who loved the same man, lamented aloud, in each others arms.

Agnes Taylor wept because of the guilt and the anguish she felt when she came into the presence of the woman whose husband she had been sleeping with most of her life, and had even borne his children for him. Now, this same woman who should have been rejecting her, was accepting her into her home, and comforting her in her arms in her time of need.

For Emma Jean, forty one and a half years of disappointed misery had finally climaxed in a deluge of diversified emotions.

WARD STREET

For forty two years she had been married to William Bernard Stone, nicknamed, 'Buddy;' most folks called him Mr. Bud. Emma Jean loved her 'Buddy' so much. Oh, how she had longed to make him happy.

At the beginning of her illness she pleaded with him to divorce her. She wanted him to be free of her, and the pain and self denial she knew he would have to suffer because of her. Mr. Bud refused the divorce because he loved his wife. He proved it by personally, taking care of her himself. He never considered having her committed to a nursing home. Now, the very woman who had been the wife and mother for her husband that she could not be, was being sheltered in her arms.

Over the years, many had consistently brought her reports that Agnes and her husband were lovers. She had refused to believe or accept the truth, although she realized that her husband needed a woman. 'Why...?' she questioned. 'Why does life have to be, so? Why does life have to be cruel? Why couldn't life have been better for Buddy and me?'

WARD STREET

All the questions, disappointments, agony, frustrations, self-pity, misery, hatred, hopelessness and reality had now surfaced and flooded her soul. The walls which she had built over the years to fortify her sheltered emotions, were now overflowing.

Mr. Bud was not a weak man. In fact, he was known and respected for his strength. Yet, what was taking place in Emma Jean's bedroom, was more than he could endure. His heart broke, and his knees buckled underneath him. He slid down the side of the door frame to the floor, and squirmed around, mumbling incoherently. His knees were drawn underneath his chin, positioning his body in the form of a fetus. To see the only two women he ever loved in such a pitiful condition, had caused his mind to go into spasmodic convulsions. All the years of pent-up guilt and pain in his soul, which had lain dormant for over forty years, had ultimately, emerged with the sudden violence of an erupting volcano.

As Mr. Bud laid on the floor in this awful moment of regret, he tried urgently, to dispel the

WARD STREET

guilt and abhorrence of the past. The disorderliness of his mind prevailed, sending pivoting mental images from one fragment of his unhallowed life to the next!

'She, knew!' he realized, as his mind went back to when he had come home after making love to Agnes that first time. Yes, Emma Jean had known. Her searching eyes, and questioning expressions, told him that she knew he had been unfaithful to her, although she did not accuse him. Looking back over the adulterous years that he had lived during his marriage to Emma Jean, he recalled the same emotions that she displayed the first time, was the reaction as always when he came into the house after sleeping with Agnes. And even though she never said anything, he knew he had hurt her.

Marriage Is Symbolic Of The Church

Wives, submit yourselves unto your own husbands, as unto the Lord.

WARD STREET

For the husband is the head of the wife, even as Christ is the head of the church: and he is the saviour of the body.

Therefore as the church is subject unto Christ, so let the wives be to their own husbands in every thing.

Husbands, love your wives, even as Christ also loved the church, and gave himself for it;

That he might sanctify and cleanse it with the washing of water by the word,

That he might present it to himself a glorious church, not having spot or wrinkle, or any such thing; but that it should be holy and without blemish.

So ought men to love their wives as their own bodies. He that loveth his wife loveth himself.

For no man ever yet hated his own flesh; but nourisheth and cherisheth it, even as the Lord the church:

For we are members of his body, of his flesh, and of his bones.

For this cause shall a man leave his father and mother, and shall be joined unto his wife, and they two shall be one flesh.

This is a great mystery: but I

speak concerning Christ and the church.

Nevertheless let every one of you in particular so love his wife even as himself;and the wife see that she reverence her husband.
Ephesians 5:22-33.

For the first time in his life, Mr. Bud admitted,and accepted the true fact which he had recognized years before;that there is a bond set between a man and a woman who are married to each other that binds them together.When the bond is broken because of infidelity, the spirit of the offended party knows it, although no accusations are made. The reason why; the offended party refuses to accept the truth. Man, is capable of accepting or rejecting whatever he wants to. Refusing to believe painful truth, temporarily minimizes reasoning, which causes reality to become more tolerable!

The Social Worker

A persistent knocking at the door brought Mr. Bud to his feet.

WARD STREET

Realizing that someone was at the door, he reluctantly staggered down the stairway, pausing every few steps shaking his head, trying to clear the film out of his brain.

When Mr. Bud got to the door, two husky white police officers were standing there, accompanied by a sturdy looking colored woman who introduced herself as a nurse and social worker. Mr. Bud stood swaying awkwardly, with a questioning expression. "What can I do for you?" he muttered, drying his eyes on his sleeve.

"We were told that we could find Agnes Taylor, here," the social worker replied politely. "It seems she may need help."

"Well, she was a little upset awhile ago," Mr. Bud said uneasily. He eyed the police officers and the social worker suspiciously. "Everything is under control now."

The social worker smiled. "Could we see her?"

Mr. Bud made a gesture, letting everybody in. "She's up the steps, there," he said. "Go right up."

"You go first," the social worker suggested. "You lead the way."

WARD STREET

Mr. Bud led everybody up the steps, leaving the door open. Emma Jean and Agnes Taylor were still in the comfort and security of each others arms when Mr. Bud came into the room with the officials.

"What...what do they want?" Emma Jean asked, puzzled. She turned her attention away from Agnes Taylor to her husband. "Why are the police here, Buddy? What do they want?"

"They are here to see Agnes. They want to help her." Mr. Bud put his arm around Agnes, and led her over to where the social worker was.

"But...why?" Emma Jean insisted.

"She'll be alright," the social worker assured her. "We'll take good care of her."

Mr. Bud displayed mixed emotions. "You'll take care of her? You are not taking her anywhere, are you?"

"We have to take her downtown for observations," one of the officers spoke up. "Normal procedure for cases like this."

"She'll be alright," the other officer said. "In most cases a patient is just kept over night."

WARD STREET

"You are not taking her anywhere without her clothes," Sarah said. She had come up the stairway, and into the bedroom with a traveling bag. "Buddy, I'm the one who called for help. I'm sure I did the right thing. I believe Agnes need to go somewhere and rest for a few days. You and these officers leave the room until I put Agnes' clothes on her."

"Thanks, Sarah," Mr. Bud said, leaving the room with the officers. "I'll go downtown with her when you get her ready."

Predator

"Nel, somebody is looking in the window." Rodney had come quietly into the room where Nellie Mae had fallen asleep, rocking Rachel. Her hand was merely resting on the cradle. Rodney, conscious that Rachel was sleeping, spoke in a whisper, close to Nellie Mae's ear. "There's a man out there."

Nellie Mae's eye's fluttered open. "Wh-what? Who...who is it?"

"I don't know who it is, but he's looking in the kitchen window."

Nellie Mae eased off the sofa, pressing her fingers against her lips. "Sh-h-h. Let's go see."

The man started grinning contagiously, when he saw Nellie Mae and Rodney approaching the window. Nellie Mae raised the window just enough to hear what the intruder had to say.

"What do you want?" she asked. "Who are, you?"

"Jesse James Pritchard."

"O-o-oh! So you are Jesse James Pritchard? I thought you were in jail."

"I wuz. They turned me loose t' day. I killed a man, yuh know. I cut'im t' death."

"So I heard. You didn't have to pull all of your time, I see."

"They let me out fur good behavior. Where's Phoebe?"

"You haven't heard? Phoebe's dead...oh, you've been in jail, though. That's why you didn't know."

Jesse James Pritchard stopped grinning, and his mouth dropped open. "Phoebe...dead? When? How?"

"Her brother, Jesse, tried to get rid of that baby of yours, and she died."

WARD STREET

A fit of anger flashed across Jesse James Pritchard's face!"Why would J. want t' do some'um like that? Man...I loved that woman! Why would he wanta git rid'a my baby? I can't b'lieve this!"

"J. just didn't want her to have your baby,"Nellie Mae sneered, lifting her chin with an air of dignity, looking down her nose at Jesse James Pritchard."He felt for sure Phoebe could do better than you. We all felt that way!"

"Yeah!" Rodney added defiantly.

Jesse James Pritchard was very successful in concealing his emotions, but something in his eyes told Nellie Mae that she and Rodney had said the wrong thing to this man. He was not pleased at all. "Where is, J.," he muttered through the gap in his teeth, after a moment of silence.

"In jail!"Nellie Mae yelled impatiently. "Where you ought to be!"

Jesse James Pritchard was grinning again, but his eyes had become like cold steel! "Is there anybody else I kin talk t'? I don't think I like yuh."

"There is nobody else in this

house but me and my babies!" Nellie Mae shouted. "Now get away from my window before I have you locked up again!"

Jesse James Pritchard fastened his icy stare upon Nellie Mae and Rodney and backed away from the window. "Tell J. I'm gon' git'im fur what he did when I see'im. I'll be waiting fur'im when he gits outa jail."

Nellie Mae watched boldly until he reluctantly got out of the yard, and disappeared down the ally. Jesse James Pritchard was more angry than ever now. To have suffered total rejection by Nellie Mae, and to have learned that he was also looked upon with disdain by the family of the woman he loved, indisputably, added more fuel to the fire of hatred and resentment, that was already burning in his soul. A long burning fire, kindled by a life of rejection because of his negative attitude, and his hostility towards society. Jesse James Pritchard had failed to realize, that to make friends, he would have to show himself friendly. Even then, he would not be adequately loved and accepted by everyone. Not learning

WARD STREET

to conform to rules and laws which govern society; not striving to get along with those he encountered, Jesse James Pritchard lived a life of habitual violence, which had become a part of his nature.

The man he killed in the crap game, appeased the malice in his soul for a season. Now, he was more hostile than ever! Jesse James Pritchard moved out of the allyway, and around the corner to the front of Nellie Mae's house. He walked directly across the street and stood menacingly, glaring hatred at the house for a time. Then, drifted aimlessly down the street, ironically, towards Mr. Bud's house.

When he had left the house for the police station with Agnes, Mr. Bud had left the door of the house open as he usually did, so that the children could come in and see Emma Jean when they wanted to. The children in the neighborhood loved his wife dearly. Miss Emma Jean, they called her.

When Jesse James Pritchard came abreast of the house, by chance, he noticed that the door was ajar. Without hesitation, he went on in. He paused when he reached the stairs, then, crept up the steps.

Taking it for granted that the foot steps on the stairs were Mr. Bud returning from the police station, Jesse James Pritchard's entrance was unnoticed by Emma Jean and Sarah. Within seconds, Jesse James Pritchard was in the doorway of Emma Jean's bedroom. Sarah, attending Emma Jean at her bedside, noticed a change in her countenance, and followed her gaze to the intruder in the doorway.

"What are you doing here?" Sarah asked. "What do you want? Who are you?"

Jesse James Pritchard was grinning again, now. "Jesse James Pritchard," he said.

"Jesse James Pritchard," Sarah said, perplexed. "Jesse James Pritchard...name sounds familiar."

"What are you doing in my house?" Emma Jean wanted to know, breaking her silence. "You don't have no business in here!"

"Jes' checking out this pretty lady, heah," he told her sarcastically, turning his attention towards Sarah. "Checking out this fine lady."

WARD STREET

Sarah was eyeing him suspiciously, now. "Are you the same Jesse James Pritchard that caused my niece all that trouble?"

"What niece? What trouble?"

"Phoebe, that's who."

Jesse James Pritchard stiffened, the grin faded, and was replaced by a sneer. The eyes, which are the mirror of the soul, reflected his true feelings towards Sarah, after learning who she was. Again, bringing to surface every misguided word that had ever been used against him; every insult, every painful put-down, and every other unpleasant rejection which was dormant in the crevices of his heart. Now, as always whenever he was opposed, his first instinct was to fight back; retaliate; hurt somebody!

The most fearful expression ever to be imagined, came upon Jesse James Pritchard's countenance, then dimimished, leaving his eyes two narrow slits of fire! As he moved about the room, his actions took on a certain cunningness, like that of a catlike animal; a tiger, leopard or panther, just before pouncing upon it's prey.

"My name is Jesse James Pritchard. An' I'm jes' as bad as my name is. I already don' kill me one nigger. I'm gon' kill me two mo' 'fore I leave heah t'day. I'm gon' git me some lovin' from this heah fine pretty lady heah first, though. I heard 'bout yuh. Phoebe tol' me 'bout yuh. Yea, yuh niece. Never had a man, huh? Well...yuh gon' git one t'day. I'm gon' giv' yuh some'um t' make yuh smile. Haw, haw, haw, haw, haw!"

What Jesse James Pritchard had said, and his crazy laugh, sent chills up and down Sarah's spine. She did not dare even for a moment, allow him to suspect just how frightened she really was. Sarah, being a God fearing woman, recognized what he was. She knew that this man had allowed himself to become possessed by the Devil. Over the years she had prayed for, and delivered many such as he. This man could be saved also, if he wanted to be.

Sarah groaned within herself, longing for help from Heaven! 'O-o-oh! If man, who is made in the Image of God, would only turn to Him in time of need...when he was in trouble; how much sweeter life would be. God, Who is no re-

WARD STREET

specter of persons, can, and will fix a corrupt heart, if it wants to be made whole. But God will not intrude upon anybody's will. And, is there a limit...a point of no return? Can one allow oneself to go so far into the depth of darkness, until even God cannot reach him? Is it possible?'

Jesse James Pritchard's grip was like a vice upon Sarah's arms. She knew that she would not be a match for this man. As she felt his hot stale breath upon her cheeks and neck, she began pleading the blood of Jesus. She fought him off as best she could, but could not prevail.

The struggle caused Jesse James Pritchard to become more savage, bringing out the worse in him. He tore and ripped her clothes until her breasts lay bare. Sarah was a beautiful woman, and even though middle aged, her breasts stood out smooth and firm. She was a virgin, and no man had ever touched her body, or looked upon her nakedness as this man had done, not to mention make love to her.

At the sight of Sarah's nude breasts, Jesse James Pritchard became more aggressive, and buried his face deep into her bosom, kissing and slobbering over her.

The situation was almost out of hand, and Sarah knew she had to retain her composure and out wit this man. Her only hope she reasoned, was to make him kill her. She had never had a man, and she was not about to start now, not with this animal. She would rather have him take her life!

When the struggle had begun between Sarah and her attacker, Emma Jean had started a struggle of her own. She had been trying to drag her crippled body over to the nightstand, that was near her bed. Finally, she reached it. As she fought the terrible pain that dominated her body, the only sound that came up out of her throat was a barely coherent, "I have to help Sarah. I have to...I have to. If I can only...help Sarah." With almost her last bit of strength, Emma Jean managed to pry open the drawer to the nightstand, and began fumbling inside.

Jesse James Pritchard did not ease his grip on Sarah, but she sensed his sexual interest lessen, as she bombarded him with insults. "You are, nothing!" she taunted. "And after you take me, you will still be nothing! You pig! Dog! You stupid...ignorant fool! How dare you put your stupid,filthy mouth on me! How dare, you! How dare, you!"

Grinning again, Jesse James Pritchard loosened his hold on Sarah and became motionless,as if trying to decide what to do next. Sarah realized that in a moment, he would have made up his mind.To help him decide, and possibly get what she wanted, she spit on him! The grin disappeared,and his eyes told Sarah that she was going to get what she had been asking for.

Almost instantly,a straight razor appeared in his hand, and Sarah could feel her flesh being ripped and slashed! Especially, her face!He seemed to want to mar her beauty, more so...to disfigure! Sarah turned away, shielding her face and breasts as best as she could. Jesse James Pritchard began slashing her in her back, making deep gashes in her flesh!

Sarah found that she could no longer stand up, and felt herself sinking to the floor, sensing vital organs had been severed. Just before she lost consciousness,she was aware that Jesse James Pritchard was reaching for her throat with the razor. Then, she heard the sound of gunshots, and the smell of gunpowder filled her nostrils. The odeal was over!

Foreboding

  Mr. Bud's mind was numb from exhaustion as he drove home from the hospital. He and the police officials had taken Agnes Taylor there for observations. The hectic events of the morning had taken their toll on his nerves. But there was one relief. He knew that Agnes had been secured. The doctors at the hospital, after their preliminary examination, told Mr. Bud that Agnes needed a rest in the state mental institution for awhile, and assured him that she would be alright.
  As Mr. Bud neared his neighborhood, he felt a sense of foreboding. When he turned the ol' cadillac into Ward Street, he found that he could not get anywhere near his house. The crowd, police cars and ambulances had

WARD STREET

Ward Street completely blocked. He stopped the car in the middle of the street, and walked the rest of the way on foot.

When he got closer, he could tell that the commotion was at his house. Approaching two uniformed police officers, he identified himself. They dispersed the crowd, and let him through.

Mr. Bud could not help but notice that many of the women and children wore tear stained faces, and the men shifted their glances towards the ground when he walked past them. It was needless to question anybody, for their reactions had already told him that something dreadful had happened.

When Mr. Bud got upstairs to the bedroom, it was set up like a hospital room. Sarah was lying on the floor, breathing with the aid of an oxygen mask. She had been stripped naked by the doctor and the nurse. They were working on her, putting stiches in the gapping wounds which covered most of her body. The ambulance crew attended the oxygen tanks and the blood.

Jesse James Pritchard's body was lying on the floor next to

WARD STREET

where Sarah was being worked on, still holding the razor in his grasp.Nobody had even bothered to cover him up. His head was lying in a pool of blood which had oozed up through his mouth and nostrils, indicating that he had drowned in his own blood.

Bessie Moody sat grief stricken. She was in a rocking chair beside Emma Jean's bed, rocking franticly,staring out into space. Transfixed! Mr. Bud started to speak to her, but bit his lip instead. Choking back a sob, he let his hand rest on her arm for a moment. Then, he turned his attention to the bed where his wife lay covered. She was motionless, and he dreaded what he knew he would find there. He lifted the sheet and pulled it back. Emma Jean had died still gripping the 38-revolver in both her hands.Her eyes were open, displaying the fright and anxiety she had suffered, struggling to save Sarah's life. Shaken at what he saw, Mr. Bud mourned, softly. He regained his composure, kissed Emma Jean gently, and closed her eyes.

A plain clothes policeman came over to the bed where Mr. Bud was. "Don't touch that gun," he said. "We need it for evidence. We don't want anybody else's prints on that gun but hers. That gun was used to kill that man over there on the floor."

Mr. Bud was about to pry the gun out of Emma Jean's lifeless hands, but he obeyed the officer. He shoved both hands into his pockets, and moved away from the bed. Mr. Bud was surprised that the ol' gun would even fire. It had been in the drawer of the dresser for so long, he had nearly forgotten it was there. He had bought the gun for the house many years before. It had never been fired, until now.

'What a tragedy,' he thought. 'Emma Jean had to be the first to fire that gun...killing a man!'

"Oh, the agony she must have suffered to get to that gun," Mr. Bud told the policeman. "That must be the reason she died. It took every bit of life there was in her body to open that drawer, get the gun in her hand and pull that trigger."

"Yeah, that's what did it," the officer agreed. "The Doc. over there examined her when we first

WARD STREET

got here. He said she died of a heart attack."

The officer took a handkerchief out of his pocket, covered the gun, pried it out of Emma Jean's hands and handed it to another officer. Mr. Bud turned his attention to Bessie Moody until the officer motioned him over to where Jesse James Pritchard's body was lying.

"Your wife sure did the human race a great big favor when she got rid of that one," the officer told Mr. Bud. "He sure was a mean one. He loved cutting people up. He slashed his way from Greensboro to Baltimore with that razor. She fixed it so he won't be cutting on anybody else."

"Who was he?"

"Jesse James Pritchard."

"So, that was Jesse James Pritchard."

***

WARD STREET

CHAPTER-12

REUNION

What? Know ye not that he which is joined to a harlot is one body? For two, saith he, shall be one flesh.
I Corinthians 6:16.

Months had gone by since Emma Jean had died, and this was Mr. Bud and Agnes Taylor's wedding day.

Although Emma Jean was no longer alive, Mr. Bud would never stop loving her. Agnes Taylor was the mother of his children, but he had never loved her the way he loved his wife. Agnes Taylor was quite aware that Mr. Bud loved his wife more than any other woman, which added to the love and respect she had for him already. It made her proud to have shared her bed with him all those years. She never considered herself just another adulteress, whore or harlot, but the mother of his children, that his wife could never have for him.

For a while after the death of Emma Jean, Mr. Bud had lost the will to live. Sarah, being there when he needed her, is what kept him going. Her prayers and encouragement brought him out of the state of depression he was in. Sarah had been healed psychologically of the damage which the ordeal with Jesse James Pritchard had left, but the scars in her body were still there. The razor had left her body disfigured, and she was now in a wheelchair. Jesse James Pritchard had done his job well.

During her recovery, Sarah urged Mr. Bud to pursue and renew the relationship with Agnes Taylor, which had declined over the years for some reason. "She will be good for you," she insisted. "It will be good for both of you to get together again. After all, Agnes is the mother of your children. Go and see her. Get her out of that place she's in. That institution is no good for her."

Because of Sarah's advice and persuasion, Mr. Bud started visiting Agnes at the institution. At first Agnes was depressed when he went to see her, and was unwilling to talk to him. Most of the time when he visited her, she acted as

WARD STREET

if she did not recognize him. Then he started visiting her everyday, sharing long hours with her, around the grounds of the hospital. Agnes Taylor's stay at the institution, had caused her mind to deteriorate, but with Mr. Bud's loving care, she regained her health.

The Church was filled to capacity, and all who could not get inside were gathered on the sidewalk. It was a happy occasion for everyone to see two people whom they loved so dear, unite in Holy Matrimony.

The joy of the event was easily read on the faces of the children and grandchildren of Mr. Bud and Agnes Taylor. The bridesmaids were made up of their own daughters. Mr. Bud's best man was one of his own sons. Sarah was maid of honor, although she had to ride in her wheelchair. Nellie Mae pushed her where she wanted to go. Rodney was ring bearer.

Then, the wedding was over. Mr. Bud and Agnes went home to live together as husband and wife. The union between these two people which had begun years before, had become lawful now. Lawful in the sight of God and man. No greater union on earth can be formed than that of a man and a woman who comes together in sexual union, producing another human, made in the Image and Likeness of God with an eternal soul, whether the union is performed within the bounds of Holy Matrimony, or with a whore or harlot. When a man and a woman come together in a sexual union and a child is conceived, that means God is brought into the union. God is The Creator!

Mr. Bud and Agnes were now free to enjoy their relationship, and their children.The days of living in the shadows so that loved ones, family members and friends would not be hurt were over.

Acquired Immune Deficiency Syndrome

"Yes, this is Mrs. Billy Joe Williams." The telephone had rung and Nellie Mae was speaking into the transmitter. It had been some time since anyone had addressed her as Mrs. Billy Joe Williams. "What can I do for you?" she ask-

WARD STREET

ed the caller.

"This is the hospital, Mrs Williams. Mr. Williams is one of our patients here. When he was first brought here, he insisted he had no relatives or friends. We checked his personal belongings, and discovered your name and phone number. Mr. Williams is a very sick man. In fact, we don't think he can last much longer. However, had he been brought here sooner, maybe we could have done something for him. Could you give us some information about your husband?"

"I'm sorry, but there's really nothing much that I will be able to tell you. We haven't lived together as husband and wife for two years. How he has been living, or what he has been doing all this time, I wouldn't know. Maybe I had better come to the hospital. There may be something that I can do."

"Yes, that will be fine, Mrs. Williams. Thank you."

When Nellie Mae entered the hospital room, she paused for a moment at the foot of the bed where Billy Joe was sleeping. She barely recognized him. The name plate on the foot board of the bed, helped confirm who he was.

As she looked upon this poor suffering creature whom she once loved, the tears began to flow. She fought hard to hold them back but they flowed freely.

Nellie Mae sat down on the edge of the bed. She took Billy Joe's slender hand and pressed it to her cheek. He was awakened by her presence. When he opened his eyes and recognized her, he was too weak to show any trace of emotion. "Nel," he managed to whisper. "Nel."

"Billy Joe!" Nellie Mae cried. "How did you get like this?"

"I haven't been taking care of myself."

"But...but, why? Why?"

"After you left me, I went back to the old life. Now...this. I am sick. I am sick, and nobody knows what's wrong with me."

"I...I don't like to see you like this. I wish I hadn't come."

"I didn't want you to see me like this. That's why I lied. I said I didn't have any family or friends. Or even you. They found you, anyhow. How...how is Rachel?"

WARD STREET

"Rachel is alright. She just had another birthday. The old life you mentioned; did you mean that you went back to the gay life?"

He nodded his head.

"But...how could, you? I don't understand. You are fathering children now. You didn't have to live like that!"

"I didn't care because I had lost you."

"Nothing could ever make me go back to what I was," Nellie Mae aired a tiny trace of dignity. "God took me out of the hell that I was living in, and I am going to stay out."

"I'm not as strong as you are. You were always the strength in the family. I just couldn't make it on my own." Billy Joe turned his face to the wall.

Nellie Mae was tormented almost to a state of despair, when she recognized just how pitiful her husband was, and her inability to help him. She released Billy Joe's hand, rested it across his thin chest and stood to her feet. "I'm going to talk to the doctors before I leave," she said. "Maybe we can find out what's wrong with you."

WARD STREET

"Yes," he nodded. "Yes."

The questions Nellie Mae asked the doctors went unanswered. "But I can tell you one thing," one of the doctors said. "This disease is something new. Rare...very rare. We have never come up against anything like it before. When we first brought your husband here, we treated him for pneumonia, because he had all the symptoms. His lymphatic system showed no response to treatment. We treated him for several other diseases, including, encephalitis. We also ran tests for leukemia, which is a blood disease. Something is destroying the white blood cells. We don't know what it is. We do know one thing though, he seems to be infected with some rare type of virus."

"Doctor, how long can he possibly last in this condition?" Nellie Mae wanted to know. "He's so weak, now."

"He just keeps getting weaker and weaker. There's nothing that we can really do right now, but keep running tests. We can't treat him for any specific disease, if we don't know what it is."

WARD STREET

"You see, Mrs. Williams, there are new diseases that we come in contact with everyday," one of the other doctors injected. "Some of the diseases we are able to diagnose right away. Some...never. However, there are diseases which we encounter that may take years of strenuous research to discover a cure for. Now, in your husband's case, his immune system seems to have lost it's ability to fight off certain diseases. Why? We simply do not know. But we are still searching."

When Nellie Mae got back to Billy Joe's room, she was no less apprehensive, or any more hopeful than she was when she left. Billy Joe was asleep again. This time she would not wake him. Nellie Mae sat in a chair opposite from where Billy Joe was sleeping. She watched him while she pondered their past lives; Billy Joe's life as a homosexual. Her own life as a prostitute. 'How disgusting,' she thought. 'Trying to satisfy the sexual depraved notions and desires of those around us, and even seeking pleasure and fulfillment ourselves, while doing

WARD STREET

so. Being taken advantage of. We were so happy for a time when we first got married. Why...couldn't life have worked out for us? Didn't we deserve it? Isn't everybody entitled to a chance at life? Didn't we deserve better than what we had? Oh, God, heal his body! Fix things for us!'

Watching Billy Joe lay there as helpless as he was, Nellie Mae realized that his condition was the result of his own sins. She had to admit that both, she and Billy Joe had indisputably, allowed sin to control their lives. The words: "You can be sure your sins will find you out," were brought to memory. She was so impacted by the devastation of sin, she began shaking and trembling! She tried to constrain herself from lamenting too loud there in the hospital room, by sliding out of the chair, and onto the floor. She laid prostrate on her face before God, letting out the agony, pain, frustrations, fear, disappointments and disillusions that had lain dormant in the depths of her soul for so long. When the tremor was over and Nellie Mae was calm again, she stayed in the same position on the floor until she lost all tract of time.Nellie Mae reasoned,that it was the Hand of God which allowed her to lay there without being disturbed by any of the doctors or nurses. Or, anyone else. Finally, she got to her feet and tidied herself as best as she could. She went over to the bed where Billy Joe was, kissed him and left the hospital.

Jo-Belle

Billy Joe was being funeralized and the Church was packed. The Church was over crowded, and the sweltering heat did not make conditions any better. Most seated, were family members and friends of the family. Many had to stand. There was standing room only. Lined around the walls of the Church, were many of Billy Joe's old friends and cohorts: prostitutes,faggots and bi-sexuals. One bi-sexual in particular, and obviously a female impersonator,was crying profusely. He dabbed at his eyes, and captured everyone's attention, when his make-up, mas-

WARD STREET

cara and false eyelashes became disorganized.

One of the Church nurses was sitting next to Nellie Mae.

"That's Jo-Belle," she whispered, nudging Nellie Mae in her ribs. "That's who your husband has been living with all this time. They were lovers, living as man and wife. Nellie Mae, he has part of Billy Joe's name. 'Jo'-Belle. Isn't that a mess? Uh!"

"So, that's who Billy Joe was living with," Nellie Mae sighed. "No wonder he got sick and died. Living with a thing like that, maybe he is better off dead, after all."

When the Minister in charge of the service began speaking words of comfort to the family, Jo-Belle started swooning and swaying. Then, crumbled to the floor. One of the fags who had positioned himself to lessen Jo-Belle's fall, attempted awkwardly, and with very little success to pull Jo-Belle's skirt down to cover his thighs and knees. Deacon Sanders, coming to the rescue, took off his coat, and chivalrously, spread it over Jo-Belle's legs. The nurse nudged Nellie Mae a-

WARD STREET

gain."Can't the Deacon see that's a man? What's wrong with him?"

"Well, you know how Deacon Sanders is," Nellie Mae said."He has a big heart.He's always trying to help somebody.I will be glad when this mess is over in here. Thank God, it will soon be over."

The Minister continued with the Eulogy, but the message escaped Nellie Mae entirely. She went into deep thought. She shut out the Minister and those around her, locking herself into the private closet of her mind.Nellie Mae not only pondered Billy Joe's life as a bi-sexual, and those who were there at the funeral, but men and women everywhere that nature seemed to have neglected, not making a true choice one way or the other.

Since she had been saved, and had given her heart to Jesus Christ completely,she trusted Him without reservation. She recognized that God is not a God of confusion. He is a God of order!

God created nature,and the very essence of nature is orderliness. If it were not so, nothing would have ever existed! When God created the world He made it good, without imperfection or evil.

What corrupts, distorts and causes confusion, is sin. All men are born with a sinful depraved nature, inherited from the first man, Adam. The genetic code of the first man, has been pasted from generation to generation, down through the ages. The man carries the gene, so therefore, when Adam sinned, the genetic code in all men was affected.

'Maybe! Just maybe,' Nellie Mae almost shouted out loud. 'If only Eve had eaten of the forbidden tree and not Adam, the human race would not have been affected! After all, God did use the seed of woman to bring His sinless Son into the world!'

The payment for sin is death! Death has to pass upon all men. Nothing will ever change that. But, wait, perhaps death is not such a dreadful enemy after all. Conceivably, when God established the judgement over sin, He was setting His mercy in motion also. Mercy, invariably takes dominion over judgement! God's mercy, is why man does not have to live eternally on the earth, striving, but never being able to gratify the insatiable desires of the flesh.

Nellie Mae pondered the Scripture which says: **And the Lord God said, Behold, the man is become as one of us, to know good and evil: and now, lest he put forth his hand, and take also of the tree of life, and eat, and live forever;**

Therefore the Lord God sent him forth from the garden of Eden, to till the ground from whence he was taken.

So he drove out the man; and he placed at the east of the garden of Eden Cherubims, and a flaming sword which turned every way, to keep the way of the tree of life. Genesis 3:22-24.

The organ music and the singing of the choir, brought Nellie Mae out of her solitary enclosure. She began to cry so unrestrainedly, every tear shed, seemed to cleanse her soul of every sin she had ever committed. And she knew, without a doubt, that God had allowed her to share a portion of His Omniscience. A great weight had been lifted out of the core of her heart. She knew that all of her sins had been forgiven!

***

WARD STREET

CHAPTER-13

HOMECOMING
Sarah's Prayer

It was Sunday morning and everyone was excited. Jesse Johnson was coming home!

Five years had passed since he had gone to jail. Now he was free. Jesse was paroled after serving five years of the eight year sentence he had been given.

"Buddy and Agnes are going to take us over to the penitentiary to pick up J.," Sarah told Nellie Mae and Rodney, excited. "We are all going."

Nellie Mae eyed Sarah skeptically. "You are going too, aunt Sarah? You haven't been feeling well lately. Are you sure you can go?"

"She can go!" Rodney shouted, putting both arms around Sarah's neck. "She's going!"

"You can believe I'm going over there and bring my nephew out of that place," Sarah aired, cocking her head daringly, ruffling Rodney's hair. "Me and my wheelchair and all. J. will be needing all

WARD STREET

the moral support and prayers he can get now. Yes, I am going."

Mr. Bud took Sarah out of the wheelchair and lifted her into the back seat of the car. Nellie Mae put Rachel in Agnes' lap, and she and Rodney climbed into the back seat with Sarah. Mr. Bud put the wheelchair into the trunk of the ol' caddy, and they left for the prison.

Sarah brought Jesse home and prayed for him. She took him into the confines of her bedroom, anointed him with oil, and prayed: "O, Lord, I come before you at this time in special prayer for my dear nephew; help him, Lord, to pull himself above what he is right now. Lord, he was born into a family with a father whom he could not use as a role model... somebody whom he could not look up to and use as an example. Lord, Thou art all Powerful. Thou, Lord, can fix anything. Lord, fix it for him. Open up the doors to the medical schools, Lord Jesus, so that he will be accepted again, and finish his education, so that he can become the doctor that he

WARD STREET

has always wanted to be. Anoint his mind, Lord, so that he will be able to study and learn. But most of all, Lord, forgive him right now for his sins. Especially, for the sin of murder...for being responsible for his sister Phoebe's death. Show him, Lord, that he has been forgiven, so that he will have the courage and the confidence to go on with his life. Show him the way that You would have him to go, and what you would have him to do. Lord, he needs You, now. Help him, Lord. Please help him. This is your humble servant's prayer. And it is in the Name of Jesus, we pray. Amen."

Jesse got up from beside the wheelchair where he was kneeling. He embraced Sarah, and kissed her. "Thank you, aunt Sarah," he said. "Thank you. If The Lord will help me, I will be the best doctor I can be."

When Jesse came down to the kitchen table the next morning, Sarah could not help but notice the change in him. His countenance was aglow with excitement!

"What on earth has happened to you?" she beamed. "You are so different this morning. Whatever you have, it is catching. You are making me happy, too!"

Jesse sat down at the table with Sarah, and shared what was in his heart. "The Lord visited me last night. He showed me some things."

"Oh?"

"He showed me what he wanted me to do for Him. The Lord wants me to use my hands as a surgeon. He showed me in a dream, that I could become a surgeon, if I would obey Him. First, he said, He would change my name. He said, that He is changing my name from Jesse Johnson, to Jesse Frederick Douglass, just like He changed Abram's name to Abraham; Jacob's name to Israel; Saul of Tarsus to Paul. In the dream, I promised God that I would serve Him with my skills as best I could. When I woke up this morning I got on my knees beside my bed, and called upon God. I made a covenant with Him. I promised God, that if He would fix my mind so that I could learn and get a good education, and anoint my hands the way that I know they need to be anointed, I would serve Him 'til I die. I'm going to do it, aunt Sarah. I'm going to make it. God has already fixed it for me." Jesse knelt at the table, and Sarah prayed again, thanking God for answered prayer.

Class Reunion

"Hey, Jesse!" the voice rang out as Jesse walked on Washington Boulevard. "Jesse!"

Jesse's attention was drawn to the red convertible that had pulled over to the curb. "Richard!" he cried, after recognizing the driver at the wheel. "Rich! When have I seen you? How have you, been? Man, it's been a long time!"

"Get in," Richard said grinning, his eyes dancing with excitement. "Sit down, Jesse."

Jesse slid into the seat beside Richard and eagerly grasped his extended hand. "What're you doing in my territory, Rich?"

"Just passing through. doing a little shopping. Getting ready for the class reunion. Hey, Jesse, you should be in on this...glad I ran into you. Me and the fellas; the old bunch we used to play with: Chris, Jeff and the rest. We have been planning this for sometime. I'm sure they will want you to come."

"Yeah, I would like that. It would really make my day to see those guys again. When can we get together?"

"Few weeks from now. You've got time to get ready. Say...what'cha been doing all these years, Jesse?"

"Went to medical school, for awhile. Then, I made trouble for myself. My sister, Phoebe, she... you knew my sister, Phoebe, didn't you, Rich?"

"You told me you had a sister, Jesse. I never met her."

"Well, anyhow, she got pregnant. An unwanted pregnancy, of course. Phoebe was only thirteen, and too young to be having a baby. Plus, the father of her baby was no good. Rich, I took what little knowledge I had, and aborted her baby, and she died. To put it bluntly, I killed my sister. It's been pretty rough for me ever since. I've only been out of jail three weeks. Man...it's great to be free."

"Jesse, I'm sorry to hear this. What are you going to do now? Is there anything I can do?"

"Maybe you can help me, Rich. But first, I'm going to change my name. Once that's taken care of, I'm going back to school if I can find one that will take me. I have a serious charge against me in the medical profession now, Rich. My hands are dirty."

"My dad may be able to help you, Jesse. He knows a lot of important people in the medical profession."

"Your dad just might be who God will work through to help me. God told me that He would fix things for me."

"Jesse, after the class reunion, I will let you meet my dad. it takes many years of study and hard work to become a doctor. It's too bad that you have wasted all that time in prison. But if you continue to study hard, you can still make it. I have to study more myself. I'm going to be a pediatrician like my dad."

Jesse got out of the car, wrote on a piece of paper and handed it

WARD STREET

to Richard."Rich, here's my phone number. Gimme yours."

Richard wrote on the same piece of paper Jesse had given him, ripped his part off and handed it back."See you ol'buddie,"he said, and roared away from the curb, leaving Jesse waving.

When the day came for the class reunion, Jesse boarded the bus with confidence,void of any base, or apprehensive feelings. His spirit was lifted to a higher level when he met Richard.

Being in prison five years had not helped his self-esteem much. Whatever self-respect he had when he went to prison was shattered, because of the disappointment and disgrace he had brought upon family members and friends. But now, he felt much better about himself since Richard had invited him to the class reunion. He felt accepted.Jesse was invited to the class reunion, but he had never gone to school with anyone there. The fact that he had been asked to come,was enough to support his self-esteem.

He had been born into a world of skepticism; being treated by white folks as if he could never achieve anything, or would never be able to think for himself because he was a colored boy. In the final analysis of himself, Jesse concluded that he was his own worst enemy, because he had become so sensitive to criticism, prejudice and bigotry. He had not only suffered because of the superiority that white folks held over him, but his own race...colored folks; the negativism that his own race had injected into his spirit because of inherited inferiority which had been handed down from generation to generation! To overcome such massive skepticism, Jesse knew that he would have to conquer the enemy from within; himself!

When Jesse got off the bus, he had to walk two blocks from the bus line, over to where the class reunion was being held. When he was almost there, he could see the banners and streamers flying in the distance, and the music was blaring in the background. Smiling familiar faces greeted him when he entered the doorway. They embraced him, and pinned badges and ribbons on his lapels.

As Jesse moved away from the

main entrance and into the auditorium, mingling with the crowd, he became aware that he was the only colored guest there. He got the feeling that he had just broken the color barrier. He was ill-at-ease, and accepted his surroundings as a discomfort zone, until he heard Richard Davidson's familiar voice approaching. "Jesse, glad you could come!"

"Rich!" Jesse turned and hugged him. "Yeah, I made it. I'm here. Let's go round up the ol' gang."

Christopher Lynch was not hard to find. In fact, he found Jesse and Richard. "Hey-y-y, this guy got to be Jesse Johnson! How are you, man? It had to be The Good Lord Who sent you my way today. It's good to see you, man." Chris grasped Jesse's hand enthusiastically, and embraced him. "Jesse, you have really made my day."

"Christopher Lynch!" Jesse exclaimed excitedly. "It's been a long time, man! I know you have been doing great, because you look great!" Jesse stepped back a few paces and laughed. "Wanna know something, Chris? I'm gonna let you in on a litle secret; I always got a little nervous when I men-

WARD STREET

tioned you name...Lynch! For some reason that word bothered me." Jesse and Richard laughed good-naturedly. Christopher took himself by the necktie and crooked his neck to one side, lagging his tongue outside his mouth. All three laughed together, put their arms around each others shoulders and went searching for the rest of the gang.

Christopher Lynch had achieved his life's ambition by becoming a Minister. It was he who gave the invocation:"Grant us, O, God,that this day will not only be a success for us, but a great success. We have come together this day to fellowship, and to share with those whom we have not seen for many years. And Lord, we realize that it is God, and God alone Who can make this day work for us.For it was You, and You alone, Who, with one blood,made all men,races and color. Thank You, Lord, for life. Thank you,for being able to create life and sustain it; realizing that God is The Author of life,and not the Author of death! And the food that we are going to receive and consume while we are here, Lord, we thank You for it.

WARD STREET

Lord, this is our humble prayer; and it is in The Name of our Lord and Saviour Jesus Christ, we pray. Amen."

The food was served, the tables cleared and Richard Davidson, who was the appointed moderator, took his place on the podium. After introducing the guest speaker, who was the principal of the class of 1948, and the rest of the invited guests, he gave his own testimony. Then, advised everyone who had a testimony to share, to limit their time to three minutes. Most of the testimonies were brief, yet, interesting and exhilarating. Those who shared, told of their expectations and disappointments, successes and failures.

Then came Jesse's turn to take the podium. "My name is Jesse Johnson..." he choked up, regained his composure and continued. "Thank you for inviting me. I am not a member of the class of '48, but I do have many wonderful friends here. These were my playmates, whom I love dearly. When we were kids growing up together, we got along swell. No misunderstandings, selfishness or distrust. We shared with one another. Now, I was the only colored boy in the group, but no one ever seemed to notice but myself, of course. And I was only conscious of the fact, when I looked in the mirror. They..." The auditorium roared with laughter, everyone applauded and Jesse continued."They are indeed my friends, and my buddies. When they invited me here for this class reunion, they really made my day."Jesse turned his attention to Richard."Thanks, Rich. I needed this." Applauds,whistles and cheers exploded the auditorium, and Jesse continued. "I have had my inspirations, expectations and disappointments,too..." Jesse paused..."and failures. But I am making a come back. With the help of God and my dear friends here, I am going to make it. You know..." Jesse was interrupted by more encouragement from the audience, then continued after the applauding stopped. "...Life is like a chess game...a few wrong moves at the beginning, and life is all over before we get started: **'But thanks be to God, which giveth us the victory through our Lord Jesus Christ.'** The Scripture that I just quoted is from, **first**

WARD STREET

Corinthians, the fifteenth chapter, and the fifty seventh verse. I made such a mess of my life at the beginning, God gave me a new name. The name that I used to introduce myself when I came up to the podium, is my old name; Jesse Johnson. My new name, is Jesse Frederick Douglass."

A few applauds.

"With a name like that, I either have to change my ways, or change my name back to what it was. Now, I can't let that happen! Thank you!"

Richard got up from where he was sitting, and embraced Jesse. Everybody stood and applauded!

When the guest speaker stood up to speak, his words were brief; yet, powerful and precise: congratulatory words; words of encouragement, wisdom and humility. Then, he began to speak conclusively, "...and I am so thrilled and thankful to God, that I am the one who was granted the privilege to have served as your principal, and help establish the mode for your lives. Before I sit down, I want to say one thing more. Please, remember what I am going to say to you; God, meets all men

WARD STREET

at their own level of intelligence, and the chief end of man's education is to know God! Without the knowledge of God, we have nothing! Thank you!" The principal received a standing ovation! "One thing more..." he proceeded..."you may be seated. You know, the way that many of our lives turn out, one might think that God made man in vain. But not so! When God put man on the earth, He gave him a Book to live by..." the principal picked up the Bible from the desk..."this Book! This Book, will keep our lives from ending up on the scrap heap like an old worn out automobile. This Book, will keep us from making the wrong moves in life, as the young man mentioned a moment ago...er...er, our young colored brother here...er."

"Jesse!" Somebody shouted from the audience.

"Brother, Jesse." The principal nodded his head towards Jesse, apologetically, then continued. "If we went out and bought a brand new automobile and failed to read the manual which comes with the vehicle; or, if we did read the manual, yet, ignored the instructions on how to maintain that vehicle, it would not last. In other words, in order to keep that vehicle operating properly, we would have to read the manual, and then, don't ignore the instructions! Life, is the same way. If we want to get the very best out of this life; if we want to reap the abundance which God intended for us to have, we have to read this Book, here...the Bible! That's the way God intended it to be, and that's the way it is. Thank you, and God bless, you."

The other guest on the podium made brief statements. Richard made final remarks. Then, called Christopher to the desk for the closing prayer.

Doctor Donald Davidson

"Dad, this is Jesse. He's the one I've been telling you about...Jesse Frederick Douglass. Jesse, my dad, Doctor Donald Davidson, pediatrician."

Richard's father grasped Jesse's hand eagerly. "Whew. Great name. Jesse Frederick Douglass! How are, you, son?"

Jesse responded enthusiastically, gripping the doctor's hand. "Fine. I'm just fine. How are, you, Doctor Davidson? It's so good to meet, you. Rich has told me a lot about you."

"Well, what did you expect him to do? He's my son." The doctor laughed good-heartedly. "Jesse, make yourself at home."

The doctor had agreed to meet with Richard and Jesse in his office after regular hours, to discuss plans for possibly furthering Jesse's medical career. Jesse had entered the office with apprehension. But now, because of the warm reception, he felt more at ease.

During the trial for Phoebe's death, the testimony that Doctor Saltzman gave against him there in the courtroom, shattered all his dreams of ever being able to practice medicine. Now, he had gained more confidence.

"Jesse," the doctor began. "Richard has been telling me that you have created quite a problem for yourself in the medical profession."

"Yes, I have, sir," Jesse said.

WARD STREET

"I've been hoping that you might be able to help me."

"Well, first of all, I wouldn't worry too much about what Doctor Saltzman told the court. He's not even in the medical profession any longer. He has retired. I'm going to advise you to go back to school and finish your education. By the time you do that, Saltzman should have even less to say about the matter. When you get out of school, come and see me. Saltzman is not the only one who can pull strings in this town. I can pull some strings, too. Ok?"

"Sure, Doctor," Jesse said. "Thank you."

"One thing more, Jesse. I would like to tell you something. Something for you to always remember. You see, when I decided to become a doctor, I wanted to be a pediatrician. That way I could help God preserve life. When we abort a child, we are helping Satan destroy life. I am going to help you. But, you've got to promise me that you will do all within your power to preserve life, and not destroy it."

Jesse's countenance took on a seriousness that would have shattered all doubt of his truth and sincerity, in the mind of the most stubborn of skeptics. The earnestness in his voice was just as convincing. "Doctor, the nightmares I've had since my sister's death, have more than convinced me never to perform another abortion, or take a human life any other way. Doctor..." Jesse got to his feet... "just talking to you has given me the support and initiative that I need to get going again. Thank you."

***

WARD STREET

CHAPTER-14

DOCTOR J.
Anna

It is now, 1967, and Jesse is standing outside his new office with Anna, his fiancee. They were admiring the freshly painted lettering on the door. Jesse had completed his medical studies, plus five years of surgical training.

Jesse stood there in his new work clothes: a smock, and a stethoscope draped about his neck. He had his arm around Anna's shoulders, and felt a sense of pride he never had before.

To make this moment a reality, had taken thirteen years of study and hard work. The sacrifice and commitment Jesse had made to become a gynecologist and a surgeon, had been worth it. He was now, Doctor Jesse Frederick Douglass!

Anna slipped her arm around Jesse's waist, as she read the words printed on the door aloud; "Doctor J. Frederick Douglass!" She snuggled closer, and confidently into Jesse's arms. "I'm

WARD STREET

proud of my doctor, and I love him just as much as I am proud of him."

"Thanks," Jesse told her, kissing her full on the mouth. "I needed that."

Jesse and anna had met during Jesse's final year in medical school. Anna had already earned her degree, and was working as an elementary school teacher. She wanted Jesse to marry her when he graduated from medical school, but he refused.

"I have to finish my training and become a surgeon, he told her. "If I marry you now, something may go wrong. Children might get in the way. Then, I wouldn't be able to finish what I started out to do. Without my education, I will not be able to make the kind of life that I want you to have." So Anna waited.

'Til Death Do Us Part

Today is the first Saturday of June, 1967, and a very special day for Jesse and Anna. A day which they had long waited for.

WARD STREET

The Wedding processional was over, except for Anna being escorted down the aisle by her father, while flowers were strewn in their pathway. Jesse waited patiently at the altar with his best man, and Sarah seated in a wheelchair, who was maid of honor.

The mother of the bride, stood near the bridesmaids beaming. With a wide grin spread across his face, Reverend Williams motioned for Jesse to take his place with Anna when the march was over, and her father moved away from her side.

After the vows were taken, Jesse and Anna knelt together at the altar for Holy Communion. "'Til death do us part," they whispered, as the cup was shared. "'Til death do us part."

The Practice

By the latter part of 1968, Jesse's practice and reputation had already spread throughout Baltimore, and surrounding cities. It had only been a little more than a year since he had began

WARD STREET

practicing medicine, so he could only attribute his rapid success to hard work and dedication. Anna made her contribution of course, with positive suggestions, and consistent inspirations. Plus, the fervent prayers of his aunt Sarah. God always keeps His promises, too. He had told Jesse that He would be with him, if he would only obey.

Doctor J. Frederick Douglass had become notably popular. Everyone knew him better as: "Doctor J.!"

As time passed, Anna discovered that Jesse was giving his life to his practice, and was neglecting her. Anna loved Jesse, and was more than willing to bear the burden of loneliness, for his sake. She sympathized with her husband because she reasoned, that the real purpose for his unrelenting devotion to his work, was because of the extreme guilt he had to endure because he was responsible for his sister Phoebe's death. Anna also believed that he had set his face like flint, to prove void the critical notion, that a colored man could never achive anything. However, as the

WARD STREET

lonely years multiplied, Anna became aware of the fact that her husband's guilt and ego were not the only reasons he put so much effort into his practice. He was also greedy for wealth and fame!

It is now, 1979. Anna knew that she had put up with enough. "We have been together twelve years," she said, when she confronted Jesse. "And we have enjoyed not one single year of reasonable marriage. When are we going to have some time together? We don't have any children; no friends; we don't even have each other. What are we living for? What are we waiting for, another life? We have a fine home...er, house that is. We don't really have a home. We have cars, and plenty of money. When are we going to start enjoying all this? When?"

Although Anna had made it quite clear that she was disappointed with their relationship, and even frustrated with life itself, Jesse appeared quite sober. "I thought you wanted what I wanted. So I took it for granted that you were happy. All I've done; the study; the hard work and accumulating, I did for you...for us."

"I believe you mean well, Jesse, but all the money in the world can't take the place of love. I know welfare people who are happier than we are. They don't have a care in the world! How I envy those people. They have everything, and we have nothing!" Anna folded her arms and turned her back on Jesse in disgust!

"I knew that I weren't paying as much attention to you as I should have," Jesse told her seriously. "But I was not aware that I had been neglecting you this much." Jesse took Anna in his arms and tried to make love to her. His efforts were useless. Anna rejected him. "No. No, Jesse. We have to wait awhile for this. There's nothing there anymore. If we work at it, things can be different."

"Things will be different," Jesse promised. "You'll see. Things will get better."

But things did not get better.

After another year had gone by, Anna still did not see any change in Jesse's lifestyle. In fact, his obsession for wealth and success, exceeded all that Anna could ever

WARD STREET

imagine.

There were even rumors that Jesse was performing illegal abortions, which, Anna would not dare believe at first. But with only passive research, she found that the allegations were true. That, is when Anna decided to leave Jesse. Anna felt sorry for her husband; living with innocent blood on his hands. Murder is murder, in any form!

Anna pondered the Scriptures which point us to number three of the seven deadly sins which God hates: **Hands that shed innocent blood.**
Proverbs 6:18b.

'Why?' she questioned. 'Would J. want to live like he is living, and in the end, go to hell? Hell is such an awful place! Why? Why? J., is a good doctor. One of the best. He can excel in any field of medicine he wants to. Why this?'

"I love you, J.," Anna told Jesse when she faced him again. "But I'm leaving you. I can't live with you any longer. I am unable to live with a man who kills unborn babies, shedding innocent blood. Why are you doing this? You don't need the money."

"After I tell you the real reason why I am in the abortion business, Anna, you won't leave me. You see, as a gynecologist, I encounter many women who can't afford to have children. Especially, little young colored teenage girls...babies having babies. Some are not even teenagers, yet. After becoming repelled at what I'd seen, I decided to do something about it. I think what really caused me to become concerned, are the stories you would tell me about those hungry kids in your classroom. I remember you telling me how those kids leave home most everyday without anything to eat, and no money to buy school lunches." Jesse stuck out his chest, and gathered an air of self-righteousness. "So, there you have it. What I'm doing is not just for the money. It's for the good of everyone involved here; the young girls who would be having those babies; the poor parents who could not afford to take care of those unwanted babies; plus, we have to consider the terrible drain on the welfare system. The way I see it, unwed mothers and married parents who are unable to support their children properly, are too much of a drain on society as a whole. I believe the jails would not be as crowded if..."

"But, J., does what you just said give you the right to play God? Does it give you the authority to decide who should live and who should die? No! No, no! You are wrong, J.! Only God has the right to make that choice!" Anna's heart broke under the strain. She lost her balance, and staggered against a chair. She regained her posture and continued. "J., how could you even think like that? You are educated...intelligent. Most of all, you were brought up in the Church! You know better than this! What are you going to do now? Where do you go from here? What do you think God thinks...?"

"I believe what I am doing is right. Whatever God thinks, He thinks. I have nothing to do with that. Maybe I will have a change of heart one day. But for the moment all that I can understand, are people needing help. As a gynecologist, I am in a better position to help them than anybody else I know." Jesse paused,

WARD STREET

and glared into Anna's eyes as if to intimidate her. "Anna, if you don't understand what I just told you; then, walk right out of that door and don't ever come back."

Anna had become numb, and responded without feelings. "J., I am going to walk out of that door. But before I go, I want you to know something. I will be taking our child with me."

Jesse's mouth dropped open.

Anna's eyes were filled with amusement. "Yes, I'm pregnant. I am carrying our child. Maybe, what I just told you will shock you back to your good senses."

"Why didn't you tell me before now, that you were pregnant, Anna?"

"Do you really think that you would have had the time to listen, J.? Or to care? Are you sure you want a baby?"

"Of course, I want our baby. And I want to take care of you. Everything will be better, now. I'm sure of it. Our lives will be different. We can work it out, now."

"No, J., you work it out. I'm leaving."

***

WARD STREET

CHAPTER-15

THE PRO-ILFE ACTIVISTS
The Bombing

Anna left Jesse, and the next day after she had moved out of the house, he received a phone call from his aunt Sarah. Sarah's body had deteriorated extensively over the years, because of confinement to her wheelchair for so long. Her voice was not as strong and effective as it had been, but Jesse could tell by the urgency in which she spoke, that she could still communicate quite well.

"Jesse!"

"Aunt Sarah! How are, you? It's been awhile since I've..."

"Jesse! What's this I hear about you? Is it true, what you're doing to those little babies?"

"Aunt Sarah, listen to me..."

"No! You listen to me, boy! Anna came to see me today. She told me she had left you. She told me why. What's wrong with you? You, of all people, should know better than what you are doing. You have killed one woman getting rid of her baby. She was your own sister. I

252

was sure you learned your lesson, then! What is it going to take for you to learn your lesson?"

"Aunt Sarah, calm down for a moment will you, please? What Anna told you is true, but I have my reasons..."

"Reasons? There are no reasons for what you are doing! Don't you know that you are trespassing God's Holy law? The law that say, thou shalt not kill? Don't you realize that all of God's laws are Holy? Can't you see...? Oh, uh, o-o-oh, uh!"

Jesse heard a thud at the other end of the line. Sarah had dropped the receiver to the floor.

"Aunt Sarah! Aunt Sarah!" Jesse flickered the switch on the cradle until all could be heard was a dial tone. He then dialed emergency, for assistance at Sarah's house on Ward Street.

The ambulance crew was already at the house when Jesse arrived, and had Sarah working on her.

Jesse came dashing through the door with his black bag, and a stethoscope dangling from his neck. "How is, she?" he panted. "Is she, alright?"

"She should be alright now," the

WARD STREET

paramedic that was giving Sarah the oxygen, told Jesse, "But when we got here she was a goner. You are a doctor, I see."

"Gynecologist. I'm her nephew. I was talking to her on the phone when this happened. I'm the one who called you guys."

"Luckily, the door was unlocked when we got here. This lady live alone?"

"No. We have friends who live with her. They are not here now."

Jesse knelt at Sarah's side, and held the stethoscope to her chest. "Aunt Sarah!"

Sarah parted her eye lids just enough to recognize Jesse. Then, a fleeting glint of terror flashed across her countenance, and she walled her eyes back until only the whites showed. Then, passed out again.

The journey to the hospital was brief and intense, as the ambulance dodged through traffic with siren wailing. Jesse followed closely in his own vehicle. When Sarah was checked into the Intensive Care Unit and made secure, Jesse was permitted to see her.

She turned her masked face to the wall when Jesse came into the

WARD STREET

room. He stood by the bed and whispered her name quietly. "Aunt Sarah."

Sarah turned her face towards Jesse, but her eyes avoided his.

"Aunt Sarah," he whispered again. "Are you alright?" Jesse touched Sarah's hand, but she quickly withdrew it. She pushed the oxygen mask aside,and managed to speak between gasps."I...am afraid...of you. I can smell...the evil...in you. What...I fear... most of all...while...I am in this weakened condition...that... you might give me...mouth...to mouth...resuscitation. If that... ever happens...my prayer is that, some thoughtful person,will drive a stake through my heart...so that...I will be able...to rest in peace.It...is a terrible thing to have...innocent blood on your hands. J.,...The Lord...is going to...punish you harshly for this. I will continue...to intercede... for you, just as long...as there is breath in my body. My prayer is...that God will have mercy on your soul. Hell...is...an awful place. No one...should ever... want to go there."

Jesse knelt and buried his face

WARD STREET

in his hands on the bed.

Sarah, laid her trembling hand on his head and prayed. "O, God," she agonized, as she shook and struggled with God, with every mite of strength left in her weak body. "Save him!...Save him, for Jesus' sake! Oh, God...help him... save him from this...terrible sin! O-o-oh, have mercy, Lord!... Have mercy! Hell...is so terrible! Keep him out of that...terrible place, Lord! Please, Lord! Please, Lord! Please...oh! Uh!...Uh!... O-o-oh..."

Sarah was praying for Jesse. But he realized that now, she was fighting for her life! Jesse summoned the doctors as quickly as he could. In minutes, a team was in Sarah's room working on her, but she was dead already. God had taken her home to be with Him, where there would be no more suffering!

Sarah died praying for Jesse, but there was no change, or regret in his heart. His heart was no less hardened. Abortion became an obsession. There was no turning back.

There is none so hardened as those who have slighted the invitation of mercy and done despite to the Spirit of grace. The most common manifestation of the sin against the Holy Spirit, is in persistently ignoring Heaven's invitation to repent.

Every step in the rejection of Christ, is a step toward the rejection of salvation, and toward the sin against the Holy Spirit. Satan's influence is constantly exerted upon men to distract the senses, and control the mind for evil. He weakens the body, darkens the intellect, and debases the soul.

Jesse discontinued his normal practice altogether. He went underground to do illegal abortions. He was arrested a few times, but always managed to get off without an actual jail sentence. Perhaps the reason for that, most of his clientele were the rich and affluent.

However, Jesse did begin to receive phone calls from a group which identified themselves as pro-life activists. At first the calls were friendly, but precise, trying to convince Jesse to give up killing babies. But when he continued to ignore the calls, they became more threatening. "We know what you are doing. We plan to put a stop to it. We have warned you, and have given you ample time to quit what you are doing. Now, it's time to take action!"

"What do you want from me?" Jesse wanted to know. "Why don't you meet me out in the open so I can see who you are? I would at least like to see what my enemy looks like. Apparently, you know me but I don't know who you are. When can we meet?"

"We know who you are and that's enough. There's something else you ought to realize; we are not the enemy...you are, and we are closing you down."

"You are closing me down?"

"Yes, we are! Now hear me good, one way or another, we are going to close you down. This Killing has gone on long enough. Ok? Get the message?"

The caller hung up before Jesse could say anything further. Jesse laid the receiver in the cradle, and reclined into the big chair where he was sitting behind the desk. He sat pondering what the caller had said until he fell asleep from exhaustion.

WARD STREET

Jesse slept until the hands of the clock on the wall moved past midnight. Then, he was jolted out of the chair by the explosion. Dazed, he found himself sprawled on the floor trying to gain his wits.

The sound of the blast had come from the first floor, in the area where the abortions were performed. Immediately after the bomb was detonated, smoke filled the stairway leading to the office where Jesse was. Jesse became disoriented but managed to locate the stairway, and begin the agonizing decent through the smoke, until he was overcome by deadly fumes and crumbled to the bottom of the steps.

In the struggle to get to his feet, he became aware of the shadowy form of a man hovering over him. The man reached down and began dragging him out to safety. His appearance was concealed by a mask or a scaf wrapped about his face. Jesse could see that whoever his savior was, he had blue eyes. Just before he lost consciousness he heard the voice behind the mask, say, "I'm sorry Doc., I did't know you were still here. I thought you had left. I'm sorry. I thought you were out of the building."

Jessica Ann Douglass

When Jesse gained consciousness again, he was in a hospital bed covered with bandages. Tubes and wires protruded from his body and connected to a machine, giving him cardiopulmonary resuscitation. The burns on his body were minor, but his heart and lungs had been severely damaged from smoke inhalation.

Being a medical doctor himself, Jesse was able to evaluate his own impaired condition. He knew that he would never be the same again. In fact, he was fortunate to be alive.

Many weeks passed before Jesse was strong enough to leave the hospital, and weeks turned into months while he attempted recovery at home. Recovery for Jesse was slow and uncertain. There were moments when he was sure that his life would end. The pain and sickness in his body were almost un-

WARD STREET

bearable, but the agony that the loneliness brought upon his soul was far worse, and there were times when he wished he would die.

The paid nurse who was there to take care of him was well trained and gave him the best attention according to her ability, but what she did for Jesse was mechanical. Without feelings. She only did what she was paid to do. Oh, how he longed for Anna to be there to care for him. Even the memory of her loving touch brought comfort to his soul. If his aunt Sarah were alive to pray for him, he knew everything would be alright. She had prayed for him on her death bed there in the hospital; and maybe, just maybe...she was somewhere praying for him now.

Then, one evening when he was home alone, he was in such an awesome state of depression he wanted to end his life by taking an overdose of nitroglycerin tablets. Jesse had emptied the contents of the bottle into his hand and was reaching for a glass of water, when the phone rang. He hesitated, then, picked up the receiver. "Yes?"

WARD STREET

"This is Anna."

The voice at the other end of the line dispelled any notion of harm that Jesse wanted to do to himself now, and he felt the will to live flow into his spirit. Lips trembling, and eyes ablaze with excitement, he uttered, "Anna?"

"Is everything alright, J.?"

"It is now," Jesse said, stabilizing his emotions. "I-I didn't expected to hear from you again."

"Are you well enough to care for yourself, now?"

"Well, not really. I have a nurse that takes care of me. She's not here now. But she's here most of the time. When can I see, you?"

"I just called to see how you are doing."

"It's lonely here without you. I need you now more than ever."

"I've made a life for myself, now. You can do the same. You can..."

"Anna, I want you to know something; your call saved my life. That is, if I can call it a life. I was just about to kill myself. I have nothing at all to live for without you."

"You...you were about to kill yourself? What will you think of next? J., life is sacred. No matter what kind of a fix we may find ourselves in, we should never want to take our own life. Of course, I can understand why you wouldn't feel that life is sacred, as many precious lives you have snuffed out. May God have mercy on your soul."

"Anna, it's almost time for you to have your baby...our child. We need to be together, now. We need each other. Why don't you come on home?"

"Jesse, you know why I won't come home...the same reason why I left!"

"Anna, the old life is over now. I couldn't do another abortion even if I wanted to. I'm just too sick...too weak. I have plenty of money, now. I am a wealthy man. My wealth doesn't mean a thing if I can't have you and the baby here with me. Anna, let's give ourselves another chance together."

Anna did give themselves another chance together. She moved back into the house with Jesse, just a few days before the baby came. The baby was born a girl. She was almost the exact image that Jesse's sister, Phoebe, had been.

WARD STREET

"Maybe there's a reason for this," Jesse told Anna. "Perhaps God has given Phoebe to us again. We'll call her, Phoebe."

"No. We are going to call her after ourselves; Jessica Ann. Jessica, for Jesse. Ann for Anna. That is, if it's alright with you."

"Anna, any name you want to give her is alright with me. Just having a beautiful little creature like her in our home will bring us so much joy and happiness, a name could never make a difference. I suppose I was trying to keep Phoebe alive. We'll call her, Jessica Ann Douglass."

After having Anna back in the house, Jesse's health improved. The nurse was no longer needed. It was obvious that the presence, and the loving care he received from Anna; plus, having been given the gift of a beautiful daughter, were contributing factors to his recovery, and his desire to live. Jesse started practicing medicine again, but his commitment was limited because of the weakened condition of his heart.

The incident in the fire had damaged his heart extensively. He relied on nitroglycerin to control the pain. Jesse took nitroglycerin tablets constantly.

However, he possessed enough strength to perform secret abortions. Jesse had lied to Anna about changing his life-style, and kept this segment of his practice well concealed. He knew without a doubt, if Anna even suspected that he was aborting babies again, she would leave him. This time for good!

***

WARD STREET

CHAPTER-16

IN HIS PRESENCE
Eclipse

It is now,1986. Jesse has reached age,55. He had managed to live a fairly good life, even with an ailing heart. For some time now Jesse had become more dependent upon the nitroglycerin, and accepted the fact that his life was almost at an end.

On this particular day, December 24, 1986, Christmas Eve, Jesse had allowed his mind to take him back to Christmas Eve, 1947. He was just a young lad of 16, then. Perhaps what caused him to ponder that specific day, was the familiarity of the weather. It was raining now, the same as it was on that day in 1947.

Jesse stood at the window, staring at the traffic as it splashed through the wet streets below. The presence of the rain, had ushered his mind into the past. He lived his life again, from 1947 to 1986.

In an effort to reduce the mounting pain in his heart, Jesse left the window and went to his

WARD STREET

desk for the nitroglycerin, but when he opened the bottle he found it empty. Panicky, perspiration appeared on his brow. His palms became sticky, and his heart started pounding faster! Jesse began clawing into his chest, as if massaging his heart. Then, staggered away from the desk and fell to the floor.

Hours had gone by before Jesse made an attempt to get up off the floor. He realized that he had blacked out for he had lost all tract of time. Before he lost consciousness it was daylight. Now it was dark. The rain had stopped and all was quiet.

Jesse was aware that even his heart was quiet now. In fact, his heart was not beating at all, and he felt a peace and calm he never had before. In his attempt to get up off the floor, Jesse discovered that it was done quite easily, as if a great weight had left his body. Then, he realized that he had left his body lying on the floor. The room was filled with the stench of decaying flesh. The worms had already begun to devour the decomposed body.

In his present existence, Jesse

recognized that somehow he had acquired perfect knowledge. He was totally aware as to why his body was destroyed so rapidly. Because of the terrible, sinful state in which he had died, judgement had come quickly for him!

Suddenly, he sensed the presence of another being in the room. He found himself beholding the most beautiful of all creatures, clothed in light. Yet, Jesse having perfect knowledge, knew that he was also in the presence of the most evil being there ever was! Evil was so prevalent it was devastating! Jesse had been ushered into the presence of the one who was expelled from Heaven...Lucifer!

Lucifer, that ol' serpent the Devil, in his effort to deceive Jesse this one last time, had appeared as an angel of light! The Devil persisted with his facade by causing light and goodness to past before Jesse, transcending all deceptions. Therefore, because the very essence of Lucifer is darkness, darkness prevails, revealing his true character! Light begins to fade, overshadowed by darkness, and Lucifer's countenance eclipsed...darkness provoking light; light provoking darkness, revolving and erupting into one single cataclysmic climax, causing every evil deed that Lucifer was ever responsible for to passed before Jesse in just a fleeting moment...from Lucifer's conspiracy in Heaven, to the present! In the presence of such a being as this; one who is the master of deception, misery and suffering, and every act of confusion there ever was, the sting of death for Jesse was magnified beyond measure, and he was ushered to the very threshold of hell!There was weeping and gnashing of teeth, and misery which surpassed description!

At this particular moment,every sin and evil act Jesse had ever done; even every unworthy thought was brought before him,and he was overwhelmed by quilt and regret! He was about to be cast into the lake of fire;but somehow,he could hear his mother and his aunt Sarah praying for him. Suddenly, Jesse found that he was at the very portals of Heaven, but two huge angels stood at the gate with swords blocking passage.When a third angel came out from behind the gates with a book and checked it, he shook his head and Jesse could not enter. Jesse's name was not written in the Lamb's Book of Life! However, he was allowed to see the beauty of Heaven, although he was separated by a great gulf, and what he saw caused hopelessness and despair to multiply. Realizing that he could never exist; to share in such everlasting happiness, caused Jesse's punishment to persist even more!

Jesse was aware that Heaven was filled with Perpetual music...a continual flow of beautiful music which had no beginning and no ending. The music was in perfect harmony with all the eternal bliss, which God has prepared for all the precious souls who loved him!

Somehow, Jesse was able to recognize the fetus'...the unborn babies he had aborted; murdered, while he was on the earth. They had been made whole; completed, by The Mighty Creative Hand of God! He knew, without a shadow of doubt now, for he was receiving confirmation of what he knew to be the truth already but would never admit it: that life begins at conception!

The Power and The Majesty of God was everywhere! And Jesse was conscious of the fact that everyone who entered Heaven had to be cleansed by the blood of Jesus Christ! Even The aborted fetus' which was brought up from the earth by the holy angels to be completed by God.

Then, Jesse became aware of two precious souls who was so dear to him on the earth...his mother and his aunt Sarah. They tried desperately to communicate with him, but there was a diaphanous division, and he could not be reached.

Perfect knowledge revealed that his father, his sister Phoebe, and many of his dear friends whom he had known on the earth were there in Heaven also. Oh, how he longed to be where they were! But his yearning only manifested itself into more agony and defeat.

Then, because of the love bond between his mother, his aunt Sarah and himself, the structure that separated them was lessened; yet, remained dominant, permitting just a fragment of hope to be shared;

unfulfillment:
  Joy...yet, not joy!
  Embracing...Yet, not embracing!
  Touching...yet, not touching!
  Speaking...but, scrambled!

Suddenly, with the speed of thought, Jesse was thrust into outer darkness! It was different there. Nothing but agony, misery and contempt!

Many of Jesse's friends were there: doctors who were guilty of the same sins he was guilty of; the shedding of innocent blood. And the nurses were there, who had assisted in such heartless massacres! Most pitiful, was the unrelenting guilt, regret, condemnation and unending torment that the unrepentant mothers had to suffer, who had permitted such heinous crimes against their own bodies. Even in hell God's love is prevalent, but His standard against sin has already been set!

While on the earth, Jesse had encountered many whom had joked and made wise-cracks concerning hell; remarking that when they got there, they would be able to reunite with family and friends, or whomever, and continue the sinful, depraved style of living they had

WARD STREET

been accustomed to on the earth. But, not so! Those who were there cared less regarding anyone else. They had no relationship, or fellowship. In fact, one of the miseries that hell has to offer is loneliness. The loneliest existence there is!

The only evidence of communicating at all was done through mental telepathy, sharing their hopelessness.

Jesse recognized the Devil. But now, he did not have the appearance of an angel of light. His countenance was awful and dreadful. He laughed, jeered and clicked his heels, as he directed his imps and demons in torturing poor lost souls. It was as if he was satisfying a pleasure principle.

The same worm that destroyed Jesse's body on the earth, was in hell also. He could feel it eating away at the very center of his soul...terrifying! Like an intense internal itch, which could not be alleviated! When he found himself out of his body of flesh, Jesse was sure that he had out ran the worm that never dies, but he was wrong. He was aware that in hell, there are degrees of suffering. And for him, the worm was his highest measure of punishment. The worm was more dreadful and provoking, than the eternal fire that inflamed his soul!

And whomsoever shall offend one of these little ones that believe in me, it is better for him that a millstone were hanged about his neck, and he were cast into the sea.

And if thy hand offend thee, cut it off: it is better for thee to enter into life maimed, than having two hands to go into hell, into the fire that never shall be quenched:

Where their worm dieth not, and the fire is not quenched.

And if thy foot offend thee, cut it off: it is better for thee to enter halt into life, than having two feet to be cast into hell, into the fire that never shall be quenched:

Where their worm dieth not, and the fire is not quenched.

And if thine eye offend thee, pluck it out: it is better for thee to enter into the kingdom of God with one eye, than having two eyes to be cast into hell fire: Where their worm dieth not, and

WARD STREET

the fire is not quenched.
St. Mark 9:42-48.

Fret not thyself because of evildoers, neither be thou envious against the workers of iniquity.

For they shall soon be cut down like the grass, and wither as the green herb.
Psalm 37:1-2.

***

WARD STREET

SCRIPTURE INDEX
All Scripture Taken From
King James Version

II Corinthians 11:14............I
Psalm 119:67...................III
Psalm 24:3-4...................III
Psalm 52:1.......................4
Colossians 3:23-25...............5
Proverbs 1:7.....................5
Proverbs 4:7.....................5
I John 4:20-21...................8
Proverbs 14:34...................9
Genesis 18:17-19.................9
Deuteronomy 4:9-10..............10
St. Mark 9:42-48................13
James 1:12-15...................44
Hebrews 12:6-8..................48
Matthew 12:43-45................53
II Peter 2:19-22................54
Galatians 5:16-21...............55
I Corinthians 6:15-20...........56
I Corinthians 2:1-8.............61
St. Luke 15:4-7.................79
Psalm 136:1.....................96
I Timothy 3:4-13...............146
Ephesians 5:22-33..............189
I Corinthians 6:16.............208
Genesis 3:22-24................222
I Corinthians 15:57............236
Proverbs 6:18b.................248
St. Mark 9:42-48...............275
Psalm 37:1-2...................275